# DARK HORSE
*of* WOODFIELD

# DARK HORSE
## *of* WOODFIELD

### FLORENCE HIGHTOWER

*Illustrated by Joshua Tolford*

1962

HOUGHTON MIFFLIN COMPANY BOSTON

The Riverside Press Cambridge

Also by
FLORENCE HIGHTOWER
Mrs. Wappinger's Secret
The Ghost of Follensbee's Folly

For Josephine

# I

I⊤ WAS a warm Friday afternoon toward the end of
April. Maggie Armistead sat at her desk in Room 10 of
Henry William Armistead High School in Wolverton,
Massachusetts, but she was not attending to business.
Business was Julius Caesar as translated with close attention to syntax by Miss Eliot and the Freshman Latin
class. Maggie had already suffered through the regular
stages of boredom; from restlessness to aching, from
aching to itching, from itching to inability to keep the

eyes open, from inability to keep the eyes open to headache, and from headache, mercifully, she had passed on
into a state of trance. Sitting there at her desk, with her
eyes glazed, but open and fixed on Miss Eliot, Maggie
rode her mare Stardust over the three new jumps she
had set up in the old tennis court. Four good strides
and over the first. Four strides to the second, press hard
with the legs, a flick of the crop and over. Slow down
now, get her in hand, come up straight and quietly,
right here into a stronger canter, and now a crack with
the crop, and over the third and highest jump in perfect
form, perfectly together. There rose a sound of clapping because it wasn't the tennis court any longer, but
Wolverton Horse Show, and Maggie and Stardust, that
faultless combination, half horse, half girl, had just won
the hundred-dollar Junior Hunter Stake. The clapping
grew to a hideous clanging. Maggie and Stardust tossed
back their mane and neighed. Suddenly it was very
quiet. All eyes were upon them as was only proper,
and yet Maggie knew something was wrong. A titter
broke the quiet. Furious, Maggie turned in her saddle,
and then, all too quickly, the saddle merged into the
chair. Room 10, Freshman Latin class and Miss Eliot
closed in once more.

Miss Eliot's face was round and flat. Her customary
expression was of weary exasperation relieved by a tend-
ency of her mouth to twitch unexpectedly into a smile.
She wore her hair in a braid around her head, and the
roundness of her face encircled by the braid, combined

2

with her limp and disillusioned manner, had suggested to her students the nickname of Fried Egg.

Fried Egg, as she took shape before Maggie, seemed to have flopped against the back of her chair. One of her eyebrows had gone up in surprise, and she had apparently forgotten about it because it stayed up while her eyes wandered over the class.

"Gerald," she said to a boy in the front row, "will you please open the door to the corridor and see if by any chance a horse is trapped there?"

Delighted snickers from the class.

"Alice" — Fried Egg ignored the snickers — "you are near the window, will you look out and see if you can see a horse grazing on the athletic field?"

While Gerald and Alice reconnoitered, Fried Egg slouched in her chair as if she had just been through the ultimate in exasperation and nothing in the world could surprise or interest her now. The class, forgetting that the bell had rung, hunched forward at their desks grinning in expectation of more of Fried Egg's humor. Gerald and Alice, accompanied by further snickers, reported no horses. Fried Egg sighed, and her eyebrow came down.

"How surprising," she said in a manner that expressed no surprise at all. "I wouldn't have thought it possible for anyone but a horse to sound so much like a horse. One of you, like the famous Dr. Dolittle, has apparently mastered the language of the beasts. The language of the Romans cannot be more difficult. Per-

3

haps it is less challenging." Fried Egg sighed again. "I should like the student who has become so fluent in Horse to report to me briefly after class. Meanwhile, the assignment which I was giving out when I was interrupted is page 107, Latin to English, sentences one through ten," and so on until she dismissed the class.

Maggie pretended to be gathering up her books and notebooks like her classmates, but embarrassment (everyone including Fried Egg knew perfectly well who was the offender) and the prospect of still more of Fried Egg's sarcasm incapacitated her. She shuffled through her papers and piled and repiled her books without knowing what she did.

"If you hurry, I'll wait for you in the coatroom," whispered a passing voice.

It was Maggie's best friend, Elizabeth Prentice.

"O.K.," Maggie whispered back. She drew a deep breath and stood up. It was best to get it over with. She lifted her chin and marched boldly to Fried Egg's desk.

"Miss Eliot," she announced, "I apologize for neighing." She backed away a few steps and tossed her long black braids like an impatient horse.

Slowly Fried Egg raised her listless eyes.

"You apologize, but you are not sorry. In fact, you think you are rather clever to dispose of the matter quickly without wasting any of your valuable time."

This was so exactly what Maggie had been thinking that she caught her breath. Fried Egg overcame her lassitude sufficiently to keep her eyes open and fixed on Maggie. Maggie felt her face growing hot and red.

4

There followed a long and, for Maggie, miserable silence. Apart from general ennui, Fried Egg gave no indication of any feeling at all.

"I am sorry," Maggie murmured at last. "I am."

"You should be," snapped Fried Egg with sudden energy. "It was very rude. No one, no matter who she is, has the right to be rude to a teacher in this school." Fried Egg's eyes were now shrewd and piercing.

"I didn't mean to be rude. Honestly I didn't."

Fried Egg went limp again. "No," she remarked in her normal listless drawl, "I don't suppose you did. You were just daydreaming again."

Maggie swallowed to relieve the dryness in her throat. Fried Egg was an awfully good mind reader.

Fried Egg straightened up. "I'd like to point out that fifty years ago it may have been enough for a young lady to be able to read and write a little and manage a horse, but this is 1933. Life isn't so easy today. Either you've got to pay more attention to your studies or you've got to give up any hope of being a useful member of society." Fried Egg had delivered this speech with considerable fire, but now she collapsed again. "It makes very little difference to me, but I have a certain regard for your aunt. That's all."

Maggie muttered an awkward "goodbye" and retreated to her desk, where she carefully piled together all the books she could possibly use for homework over the weekend. Carrying these, she hurried to the girls' coatroom, where Elizabeth sprawled on the floor with her back against the wall. She was munching an

O Henry candy bar, while reading a book. She looked up.

"Did you say 'I'm sorry' nicely?"

"I said I was sorry, and then Fried Egg gave me a lecture."

"About not paying attention?" Elizabeth took a bite.

"Yes. How did you know?"

"You never do pay attention."

"I don't see why you think I don't pay attention as much as anyone else. I can't think about school subjects all the time, can I? And I don't think it's very polite of you to sit there eating that O Henry when I'm starving right in front of you, and you know I can't buy things like that because I'm saving."

"Here!" Elizabeth held up the O Henry. "You finish it. It just makes me fat. Wolfe always makes me hungry, but I can't stop reading him. It's a vicious circle."

Maggie took the candy bar. "Thanks. You don't have to give it all to me."

"Take it. Take it away." Elizabeth waved the book in a magnificent gesture of renunciation. It was a heavy volume entitled *Look Homeward, Angel*. It slipped from her hand and fell to the floor. Elizabeth flopped onto her stomach and crawled after it. "Save me from myself," she cried. "If you don't save me from myself, I'll lie down with *Look Homeward* and a bunch of candy bars, and I won't be able to get up. Like that elephant in the zoo." She proceeded to roll and writhe on the coatroom floor while emitting sounds appropriate to an elephant in distress.

6

Maggie giggled delightedly at this performance. Finally Elizabeth rose panting to her feet.

"I felt like an elephant," she explained.

"It happens to horses sometimes too," said Maggie seriously. "Look, Liz, I can't spend any money on candy and stuff to pay you back until after the horse show, but I'm going to ride Star into town on Saturday afternoon to get her used to cars and strange people. If you'll meet me here in the athletic field, I'll give you a lesson on her. I wouldn't do this for anyone else."

Elizabeth was busy stuffing *Look Homeward, Angel* into a satchel with her schoolbooks. She didn't look at Maggie as she said, "I'm sorry, but I can't."

"Why not?"

"My hair."

"So what? It doesn't take you all afternoon to wash your hair, does it? I thought you'd just washed it anyway."

"You see! You don't pay any attention to anything any more." Elizabeth gave a sniff. "The Fried Egg is right about you."

"I don't see why I have to remember every time you wash your hair, especially since you don't do much of anything else these days anyway." Maggie felt it was her turn to be righteous. "Of course, if you don't want to learn to ride Star" — Maggie swung her jacket from its hook and wafted a faint horsey perfume through the coatroom air — "it's O.K. by me."

"Star, Star, Star!" shouted Elizabeth. "All you talk about is that horse. You even smell like a horse, and

7

you don't pay attention to anything else. Not one thing. I'm supposed to be your best friend, and I told you that my father said last fall that when I had a date with a boy, he'd let me get a permanent. He just said it because I'd been pestering him so, and he didn't think I ever would have a date, and I've told you this lots of times, only you don't pay any attention to anything I say. No you don't, because just this Tuesday when Robert Appleby asked me to go to the movies with him on Saturday, I told you right off first, before anybody, because you were my best friend, and the next day I told you how when I told my father he said O.K. then I could get a permanent, and I made the appointment at Cora's because she's the cheapest for Saturday afternoon. You don't pay attention to anything but yourself and your stupid old horse." Elizabeth stamped her foot.

Maggie quailed before this outburst. Very vaguely, now, as she put her mind on it, she did remember something about Robert Appleby and Liz's hair.

"Gee, I'm sorry," she began, but remembering that Liz had insulted Star, she stiffened. "Star isn't old and she isn't stupid, and you do wash your hair all the time."

Elizabeth picked up her satchel. She lifted her chin, tossed back her hair and let her eyelids droop in the manner of her favorite movie star.

"It wouldn't hurt if you washed yours more often, Horsey," she said and swept out.

Slowly Maggie gathered up her own belongings. She felt sore inside. Everyone seemed to have turned

8

against her. First the Fried Egg, then Liz. Maggie sighed. Maybe she should have remembered about Liz's date, but Robert Appleby was just a name and a face to her. He wasn't even in the same class. Maggie set her jaw. It was too bad Liz had turned into such a pain. She used to be fun before she started washing her hair and worrying about dates. She must have washed out all her brains. Calling Star old and stupid, indeed! Maggie marched down the corridor to the front door. She made sure the schoolyard was empty before she hurried across it and down the street. To have to explain to a lot of nosy classmates what she had said to Fried Egg and what Fried Egg had said to her was more, at the moment, than Maggie could bear. As she passed Wolverton Elementary and Grammar School, she glanced over the playground to make sure that her little brother, Bugsy, wasn't waiting for her there. Seeing no sign of him, she continued by side streets toward the stable where they kept the horses on which they rode to and from school. As she turned the last corner and saw the stable up ahead, she spied Bugsy. He was crouched on his heels in the dirt, his head bent to the ground. Maggie came up close to him and leaned against a granite hitching post which, with a decrepit mounting block and a gasoline pump, stood in front of the stable. Through the open stable door (or was it from herself, and what if it was?) came a faint odor of horse which mingled pleasantly with the smells of gasoline and hot dust. Maggie drew breath and took comfort in the sun, the odors, and the familiar old stable with the two signs

9

over the door. First: CROSBY'S GARAGE AND TAXI SERVICE, and, above that, older and fainter: CROSBY'S LIVERY STABLE: HORSES FOR HIRE. Maggie smiled as she thought of Stardust waiting for her inside. They would ride home through the woods, and a whole long weekend lay ahead for schooling Star over jumps and on the road. Come Monday, which, thank heavens, was a long way off, she would have all her lessons prepared and show Fried Egg that she wasn't so bad. She'd remember to ask Liz about her hair and her date too. All would be well again. Indulgently she turned to Bugsy.

"Hi, Bugs, what's going on?"

Slowly Bugsy raised his head and trained a pair of round, black eyes on his sister. "Oh, there you are. It's war. Look." He returned his attention to the dirt.

Maggie looked and saw a ball about the size of a walnut made up of seething ants, red and black.

"What is it?" she asked, as she bent closer.

"It's a piece of candy bar," explained Bugsy. "I dropped it. The blacks spotted it right off. They live right under the mounting block. As soon as they'd started to pull it apart and drag it home, the reds spotted it too. They began charging in from down the road somewhere. It's war."

Maggie crouched down beside Bugsy. Large black ants were pouring from under the mounting block. Small red ants advanced in a column extending far down the road. It was war indeed, and most bloodthirsty. As the warriors debouched onto the battlefield, they hurled themselves at one another. Grappling ferociously, they

10

lopped off legs, heads, antennae, literally tore one another limb from limb, and in their blood lust, slashed, whacked and tore apart friend and foe alike. Small groups and pairs, locked in each other's jaws, rolled about the outskirts of the field. The ground was strewn with corpses and pieces of corpses. Here and there a headless torso stood upright, quivering horribly, or stumbled about in a prolonged and hideous dance of death. Maggie stared in horrid fascination.

"What's going to happen?"

"The reds will probably win," replied Bugsy, "but you can't be sure. When blacks are near their nest they fight harder. It can go on for hours. The reds are still throwing in troops." He leaned even closer to the ground. "Look, the reds are sending a column to attack the blacks' nest. I expect the blacks will lose in the end. The reds will cut the army off from its base, and maybe they'll collect some of the blacks' eggs to raise up for slaves. Of course," he added with the disarming modesty which only the truly erudite can afford, "I may be wrong. Ants aren't my specialty."

Maggie was more excited now than Bugsy. "Do they fight like this often?"

"Ants are pretty warlike," Bugsy replied. "Thunderstorms set them off, or just a hot day like today."

"It's terrible," murmured Maggie. "They're so savage."

Slowly Bugsy stood up. He was a short, round ten-year-old. His face was pink, his hair stuck up in tufts. His ears protruded like the handles of a sugar bowl.

11

His black eyes bugged out at Maggie. Drawing on the mine of entomological information that was his, he said with dignity, "In nature it's kill or be killed."

Maggie continued to stare at the battlefield.

"Shouldn't we start home?" Bugsy shuffled his feet. "It will go on for hours, and I thought you wanted to do some work with Star before supper. I brought along my nets this morning." He cast a quick, knowing glance at the sky. "It's on warm days in early spring that Mourning Cloaks come out of hibernation, and there might even be some new Sulphurs and Spring Azures flying around in the woods. I want to try to catch some. You can have a net too. I've got a spare."

Slowly Maggie straightened up. "Gee, Bugsy, if I didn't have so many other things to do, I'd get interested in bugs too."

"Ants are insects," Bugsy corrected her. "Bugs are a suborder, and I'm chiefly interested in lepidoptera, but never mind."

# 2

THEY ENTERED the dusky interior of Crosby's Livery
Stable and Garage. To the left of the door the erstwhile
tack room was converted to the taxi office with a telephone. Here the elder — or livery-stable — Crosby
slept in his swivel chair with the telephone balanced on
his mound of stomach and his feet on the desk. The
children went on between a double row of box stalls
variously occupied by a sleigh, a Reo truck, a Model A,
a Model T, a Chevy, an Essex, a Chalmers, and an
Electric. At the back of the stable, the smell of horse

13

which had shared the front with gasoline, oil, paint, rubber, and dusty leather rose up in force and overwhelmed all rivals. Maggie sniffed appreciatively and gave a soft whistle. Stardust's dark head with a white blaze on the forehead appeared over the gate of one of the few stalls still reserved for its original purpose. Stardust whinnied.

"Hello, Beautiful," called Maggie.

She opened the gate and, taking Star's halter, pulled her head down until the horse's cheek was rubbing her own. Stardust seized this opportunity to search Maggie gently but thoroughly for sugar or other delicacies. Finding nothing better, she nibbled tentatively at *Julius Caesar*.

"Pig!" Maggie laughed and pulled the book away. "You'll have to wait till we get home. Caesar would make you sick." She tossed all her books onto the floor outside the stall, then led Star out to saddle and bridle her.

Meanwhile Bugsy had opened the gate of the stall opposite to be confronted with the plump, spotted, and not particularly friendly rump of his pony, Pansy. Pansy shifted her weight so as to better block the entrance, and she flicked her tail in Bugsy's face. Bugsy put his shoulder to her rump and shoved until she moved enough to let him in. Yanking hard at the halter, Bugsy got Pansy's head out of the hayrack, turned her and dragged her out. While he fetched the saddle and bridle from another stall, Pansy heaved a windy sigh.

Apart from refusing to hold up her head and pretending to gag on the bit, Pansy made no fuss about the bridle, but as soon as she felt the saddle on her back, she heaved another windy sigh, swelled out her sides, and held on. Bugsy tugged at the girth straps. Pansy still held on.

"O.K." Bugsy dropped the girth. "I can wait."

He disappeared into the stall where they kept their tack and emerged, swishing two butterfly nets. Pansy was still valiantly holding her breath. Bugsy shrugged, went to the back door of the stable, slid it partly open and slipped out into a combination stableyard and parking lot. First he glanced about for butterflies. Seeing none, he approached a Franklin which stood among the parked cars. Its preposterous engine hood yawned open like the mouth of a hippopotamus, and from the mouth protruded the bottom half of a man.

"Hello, Mr. Crosby," said Bugsy.

"Is that Bugsy Armistead?" From deep in the throat of the hippopotamus the voice of the younger, garage Crosby rang out muffled, but hearty.

"That's me."

"Everything O.K.? Pony O.K.?" again from the hippo's throat.

"Yes, I'm waiting for her to let her breath out so I can fasten the girth. What's the matter with that car you're working on?"

The top half of Mr. George Crosby emerged from the mouth of the hippo. He rubbed his fat, greasy chin with a fat greasy hand. "The main thing that's wrong

15

with it is it's obsolescent." Still rubbing his chin, he gazed into the Franklin's gaping jaws. "It's obsolescent as the horse and buggy."

"What does obsolescent mean?" asked Bugsy.

"It means that it's on the way out. Time has passed it by. A few more years and this car will be an antique, like the horse and buggy today. By the way" — Mr. George Crosby turned his full attention to Bugsy — "you might tell your aunt something from me. You tell her that if she's thinking of selling that Pierce-Arrow of hers, she'd better do it quick because the Pierce-Arrow is getting obsolescent too. It's strictly on the way out. Don't ask me how I know. I just know. Right now I could give her a very good trade-in on a brand new '33 Chrysler. It's the most breath-taking model they ever put out, and Chrysler is the coming car, the car with the big future, and I'm the only authorized dealer in this part of the state. Tell her it's a chance she'd be awful foolish to miss." Mr. Crosby rubbed his chin and looked hard at Bugsy. He threw back his head and went on in an excited voice. "This '33 Chrysler's got the clean, spare lines of a race horse with courage to match. Tell that to your grandmother." He pointed a finger at Bugsy. "Tell her that if she don't believe it, she should come and see for herself. I'm getting one in tomorrow. And tell her I might be able to use that old Pierce of hers for a tow car and that's why I'll give her this specially good trade-in, but the offer don't hold for long, of course."

"I don't think we can afford to buy a new car," said Bugsy.

"Tell her" — Mr. Crosby shook his finger for emphasis — "that the only way we'll lick this depression is to spend. We gotta keep the money in circulation. We gotta grease the wheels of industry. Expansion, investment, borrowing, lending, buying, selling, spending!" Mr. Crosby waved both hands in the air and paused for breath.

"O.K., I guess I better see about Pansy." Bugsy backed toward the stable door.

"Don't forget," called Mr. Crosby as Bugsy retreated inside.

"I fooled you that time," exclaimed Maggie.

Bugsy turned to see her fastening Pansy's girth. "Thanks," he said. "Mr. Crosby got talking."

"That's O.K.," replied Maggie cheerfully. "I came out from putting on my breeches just as she was letting out her breath, and I tightened her up so quick she didn't have time to take another." Maggie slapped Pansy's shoulder, and Pansy coughed. "Honestly, Bugsy, you ought to lay into this pony more and make her behave. She gets meaner and lazier every day."

"I will. Now that the butterfly season's begun, I'll make her work."

Maggie was tucking her skirt into a pair of khaki breeches of the sort worn by Colonel Theodore Roosevelt when he stormed San Juan Hill. They were too big and had a patch in the seat. Maggie reefed them in at the waist with a safety pin, then bent to fasten some more safety pins where the buttons were missing on the legs. Next she stuffed her schoolbooks into Star's saddle-bags and mounted.

"Ready?" She turned to Bugsy, who was settling himself and his nets on Pansy.

Bugsy nodded, dug his heels into Pansy's sides, and followed Stardust out the stable door.

They trotted single file down the hardtop State road and over the railroad track. Stardust held her head high and lifted her feet daintily. In the sunlight her dark coat shimmered as if powdered with dust from the Milky Way. Maggie rode with such style and enjoyment that, despite her unconventional costume, she looked as distinguished as Star herself. Pansy and Bugsy were dowdy by comparison. Pansy had once been a neat and pretty skewbald, but greed, laziness, and advancing years had played the old Ned with both her figure and her disposition. She hung her head and sulked along, getting farther and farther behind until Bugsy clouted her with the handle of the butterfly net. Uttering an ill-tempered grunt and kicking up her heels, she increased her pace, only to slow down again as soon as she felt it was safe. If Bugsy had had his mind on horsemanship instead of butterflies, they might have proceeded more smoothly. His eyes darted over the landscape. He held one net ready to swing. The other was tucked under his thigh. Only when Pansy's pace had declined to a shuffle did he notice and remember to whack her again. Maggie turned left across the hardtop onto a dirt road which led across plowed and pasture land to a couple of farmhouses.

"Maggie!"

Maggie reined back Stardust until Bugsy, bombarding Pansy with his heels, came alongside. He handed her the spare net.

"The best place for butterflies is in the field by the Family Plot."

"Hear that, Star." Maggie made some tentative swipes with the net and restrained Star, who capered about in vague alarm at the net which she glimpsed from the corner of her eye. Maggie continued to swing the net and speak gently. "When we get to the Family Plot you can run, but you mustn't get excited about an old butterfly net. Keep steady, or you won't be able to tell a butterfly from a moth." She laughed at her own joke.

"There won't be any moths. They only fly at night." Bugsy bumped along beside Star. "Spring Azures," he commenced in his best professorial manner, "are the earliest butterflies to hatch in the spring. They are very small, and they may be any color of blue from very pale to almost violet. They fly low, and they sort of hover, and they're easy to catch. You practice on them. Leave the Cloaks to me." Bugsy fetched Pansy another clout and breathed hard. To lecture and keep Pansy up at the same time was strenuous.

"Leave the cloaks to him, Star," Maggie laughed.

"Leave the cloaks and shawls and hoods and capes and bonnets to him."

"Shut up, Maggie. There are no shawls or capes or hoods. You ought to know that." He pasted Pansy again and fixed Maggie with a round, reproachful stare. "I've a reason for wanting to catch the Cloaks myself."

"Wait a minute."

The dirt road had passed beyond the two farms and into the woods, where it became more and more overgrown until it was only a cart track. On either side notices began to appear to the effect that this was private property and trespassers would, etc. The notices were signed H. W. Armistead and were in as bad shape as the road. Maggie cantered ahead to let Star jump a sapling that had fallen across the way. Pansy trotted up to the sapling, stopped, looked at it with distaste, and, when Bugsy clouted her, heaved herself over.

"Maggie, wait!" Bugsy lumbered up beside her. "Didn't you hear me say that I had a reason for wanting to go after the Cloaks myself?"

In high spirits because Star jumped so beautifully, Maggie looked indulgently into the round eyes.

"What is it?"

Bugsy drew a deep breath. "Mourning Cloaks hibernate all winter. Now listen carefully because this isn't easy to understand, and I wish you'd go more slowly because I'm getting out of breath." He stirred up Pansy and panted for a minute. Maggie held Star back. "On warm days in early spring," Bugsy went on, "they come out and fly around and eat what they can find. In about the middle of April they mate, and in early May the female lays eggs on twigs, usually elm and willow. In about two weeks the eggs hatch into caterpillars. The caterpillars eat leaves and grow until the end of June. Then they hang themselves up and form chrysalises. The new brood of Mourning Cloaks hatches out of the chrysalises in early July. Do you get all that, or should I say it over?"

"Don't say it over. Just say why you want to catch the Cloaks yourself."

"What I want to do," panted Bugsy, "is two things."

Maggie sighed pointedly, but Bugsy paid no attention.

"I want to find the eggs that the butterflies lay and hatch them myself in captivity, only I'm not sure I can because they're so small, so I want to catch some Mourning Cloaks and keep them in cages so they lay their eggs in the cages and the new butterflies hatch in the cages, and then I'll have lots of perfect specimens and I'll sell them and get rich."

Maggie suppressed a smile. "Who's going to buy them?"

"Art and Science, Inc.," replied Bugsy a trifle smugly.

"What on earth is that?"

"It's a company that buys and sells butterflies and other insects. Scientists and collectors buy them, or jewelers that make pins out of them. I've already sold my five best Monarchs to Art and Science. I've made twenty-five cents." He glanced up at Maggie. "Of course," he added with assumed modesty, "it's nothing much, but it's a beginning."

Maggie's eyes widened with astonishment. "How did you find out about this?"

"Miss Urquhart told me."

"Don't tell me she chases after butterflies?"

"Of course not. You know how when she comes to clean she has that bag with her, and she takes papers out of wastebaskets and puts them in the bag and takes them home?"

"I certainly do," snorted Maggie. "She took all my Science notes just before a test, and I flunked it."

"You shouldn't have put them in the wastebasket."

"I didn't. They fell in."

"How was she supposed to know that?"

"Oh never mind," cried Maggie. "Just tell me what you were going to about the company that buys butterflies."

"Miss Urquhart collects pieces of paper with writing on them from all the wastebaskets in all the houses where she works, and at night she reads what's written on them, and then she puts them away. She's educating herself. It's cheaper than going to school or buying books, and anyway most books are too long." Breathless, Bugsy paused and gave Pansy another smack with the handle of the net. "She picked the advertising pamphlet of Art and Science, Inc. out of someone's wastebasket and gave it to me because she knew I collected butterflies."

22

"And you've already made twenty-five cents just selling old butterflies you had lying around?"

"They won't buy just any old butterfly. It has to be a perfect specimen."

"Why Bugsy Armistead!" Maggie shook her head with grudging admiration. "I never dreamed you could do anything as smart as that. Here I've been saving my allowance all winter, trying to save enough to enter Star in the hundred-dollar Junior Hunter Stake, and if I'd only known I could have been catching butterflies and selling them and getting rich like you."

"Not in winter," Bugsy corrected her. "You can't catch butterflies in winter."

"That's right." Maggie sighed and gazed thoughtfully at her butterfly net. "Bugsy," she asked almost timidly, "if I started catching butterflies now and sold them, would you mind? I mean it was your idea. Would I be horning in?"

"It was Miss Urquhart's idea," replied Bugsy after a minute's thought, "but I wouldn't mind. After all, more butterflies hatch in a summer than I could catch in a million years." He waved his net at the surrounding woods, and his eyes glowed with a dedicated fire. "The only trouble," he added, "is that the horse show is in June, and most of the big, showy butterflies don't hatch until July."

Maggie sighed again. "I guess I'll just have to be satisfied with entering Star in a couple of two-dollar equitation classes and forget about that hundred-dollar stake."

"Would you get a hundred dollars for winning it?"

"No, the hundred dollars is divided up, but the first prize is fifty dollars. I know Star could win the first prize. When I'm reading over the prize list — it just came out — I think about how if I had that fifty dollars, I could buy Aunt Cinny a new horse for her birthday. Of course it wouldn't be as good a horse as Amber, but it would be better than nothing."

Bugsy straightened in his saddle. His eyes bulged and gleamed.

"You know, Maggie, if we went into this together, and you earned fifty dollars at the horse show, and I earned fifty dollars selling butterflies, we could get her a good horse. Maybe we could even buy back Amber." Bugsy's eyes narrowed in speculation. "Maybe, by now, the depression has hit the people who bought Amber, and they'd sell her back cheap."

"If Aunt Cinny just had Amber back and could ride again, I'm sure she'd stop worrying about money and things, but," Maggie sighed, "I've got to have eight dollars to enter Star for the Junior Hunter Stake, and I don't see how I'll ever get it."

"Eight dollars!" exclaimed Bugsy. "That's robbery!"

"You have to enter your horse in one other Junior Hunter class before you can enter the Junior Hunter Stake. It's the rule. The other class is three dollars, and the Stake is five dollars." Maggie shrugged.

Bugsy shook his head. "How much have you saved?"

"By the time of the horse show, I'll have two dollars and eighty-three cents, and Aunt Cinny has promised me a dollar for painting the paddock fence."

"You still need four dollars and seventeen cents," said Bugsy, who was good at arithmetic. "Can't you borrow it from someone?" He paused and gazed thoughtfully at Pansy's ears while he kicked her on with his heels. "Of course, if you didn't win the Hunter Stake after all —"

"But I would. Or rather Star would. She's a natural jumper, and I'm schooling her all the time, and she's getting better and better."

"All right, but before anyone will lend you money, they've got to be sure you can pay them back."

"They can just come and look at Star. They can see how well she's built, and they're welcome to watch while I'm schooling her. If they can't be sure after that —"

"You don't understand, Maggie. This is business. They've got to have" — with an effort, Bugsy found the word — "security," he cried. "That's it. Security." Maggie opened her mouth to interrupt, but Bugsy silenced her. "What I'm trying to say, if you'll just listen, is that the unhatched butterflies in my butterfly farm would make good security."

Maggie pondered this for a minute, then gave a snort of disgust.

"Maybe they would, but who am I going to borrow from anyway? Gran won't have anything to do with money. She leaves it all to Aunt Cinny. Aunt Cinny thinks I'm lucky to be able to put Star in a couple of equitation classes. If I tell her why I want the money, it

spoils the surprise, and she couldn't lend it to me any-
way, not even with security." Maggie snorted again.
"She hasn't enough cash every month to pay the bills.
I've heard her say so."

"What about Miss Urquhart?" suggested Bugsy.

"Oh Bugsy, don't be silly. Aunt Cinny says she has
barely enough these days to keep herself alive."

Bugsy was checked, but only temporarily.

"After all she knows more than most people do about
horses, so if Star's as good as you say she is, Miss Urquhart wouldn't be worried, and if we had security like
chrysalises to show her, and if we promised to pay back
the money with interest" — Bugsy paused to gloat
briefly over his own cleverness — "she might be glad to
lend us the four-seventeen. She might consider it a
good investment."

"She might," returned Maggie, "but only because she
isn't right in the head."

"I don't see why you say that, Maggie. Art and
Science, Inc. will pay three to five cents for perfect
specimens of large, showy butterflies like Cloaks, Tiger
Swallowtails, or Monarchs."

"And how many large, showy butterflies do we have
to have to make four-seventeen?"

"At three cents we'd need one hundred and thirty-
nine, but at five cents we'd only need eighty-three and
two-fifths," replied Bugsy promptly.

Maggie laughed. "You're a whiz, Bugsy, but I'm
afraid we'd have to find someone with more money than
poor Miss Urquhart to borrow from, and I don't know

anyone who's rich enough to ask them, and neither do you."

"Miss Urquhart," began Bugsy stubbornly.

"Come on." Maggie straightened in the saddle. "Let's stop worrying about it and have a canter. See if you can make that lazy pony move."

Pansy flicked her ears and laid them back as if she understood what Maggie had said and resented it. Actually what she resented was a large, dark butterfly that was fluttering around her ears and tickling them.

3

Bᴜɢsʏ ʀᴏsᴇ in his saddle. "A Cloak," he yelled, and swung his net. The net hit Pansy on the head. Pansy jumped in consternation. Bugsy fetched her a whack on the rump that further confused her. She broke into a canter, and Bugsy headed her for the woods after the butterfly.

Frightened by this sudden activity, Stardust tossed her head, shivered, and capered about. Clucking and stroking her neck, Maggie held her back. As Pansy's rear end careened farther and farther away among the trees, Star quieted, and Maggie settled herself to wait for Bugsy's return. A moment later, another butterfly like the first zigzagged out of the woods and circled just under Star's nose. Star backed suspiciously away. Maggie caught her breath and forced herself to sit quietly stroking Star's neck with her left hand while she raised the net in her right and waited for the moment to swing. The butterfly swooped lower over the road, passing in and out of a shaft of sunlight that set its dark wings aglow with flashes of purple and amber and peacock blue. For a moment it hovered just above the road at Star's feet, displaying the lacy yellow band and, inside that, the row of sapphire spots which bordered the dark wings. It hung almost motionless in air. Maggie bent double in the saddle and swung. Star jumped, the butterfly darted into the woods, and Maggie cried out in disappointment. Thoroughly confused and frightened, Star reared. Maggie, clinging none too gracefully to Star's mane, had the presence of mind to speak gently and hold the net down while she crawled back into the saddle. The butterfly skimmed off among the trees. Maggie turned Star, tapped her with her heels, and they were off in pursuit. Star was delighted to run and, when not startled by strange flying objects, responded willingly to the pressure of Maggie's legs and the gentle guidance of the reins. They dodged nimbly between the trees and kept the butterfly in sight. But as Star swerved and turned, the saddlebags, which were carelessly packed and gaping open, began to thump and flap. From the corner of her eye Maggie saw *Julius*

*Caesar* fly out of the left saddlebag and light in a bush. A moment later, a notebook took off. It was followed by the French Dictionary. Now the saddle, unevenly weighted, began to slip. The butterfly skimmed on just out of reach. Maggie couldn't bear to let it get away. She gripped the net in her teeth, reached into the heavy saddlebag and tossed away all the books that were in it. A moment later she had hiked the saddle straight. Taking the net in hand, she urged Star on. Unaware of its danger, the butterfly darted into a little clearing and was circling again lower and lower as if it meant to light. Maggie reined Star to a sudden stop and slid to the ground. She laid the reins on Star's neck and said, "Stand."

Disappointed and more confused than ever, Star was still obedient. She followed Maggie only a few steps. Maggie lifted her net and crept up on the circling butterfly. Down swished the net, and the Mourning Cloak was a fluttering captive.

"Bugsy!" Maggie shouted. "I've got a Cloak," and in the nick of time she closed the mouth of the net.

There was no reply from Bugsy other than a pounding of hoofs and crackling of underbrush. A moment later, he galloped into the clearing, crouched in the saddle like a jockey, with his net raised.

"Where is it? It came this way." He drove Pansy round and round the clearing.

Maggie ran about, peering here and there. She spotted the butterfly as it emerged from cover of a pine tree.

30

"There, Bugsy! There it goes."

Bugsy's butterfly swooped away over a broken stone wall.

"Hah," shouted Bugsy.

He walloped Pansy and drove her at the wall. Pansy's ears went back. Maggie held her breath. Pansy galloped right up to the wall, planted her four feet, lowered her head, and skidded to a stop. Bugsy and the butterfly net sailed over the wall without her, and Maggie could have sworn that she heard Pansy laugh. Maggie ran to the wall and peered over. Bugsy was scrambling to his feet. He still gripped the net, and without losing a minute he bounded after the butterfly. It was circling now, lower and lower. Bugsy crept in close and with a swish made the capture. He folded his net over so the butterfly couldn't escape, sat down on the ground and rubbed his shoulder.

"Are you hurt?" called Maggie.

"I got him," replied Bugsy.

"Are you hurt?"

"No, I know how to fall." Bugsy lay back on the grass.

Pansy, looking smug, had already found some new spring grass growing along the shelter of the wall. Maggie grabbed the bridle and wrenched up her head.

"She did it on purpose, you know," she shouted to Bugsy. "You can't let her get away with that sort of thing."

"I know," replied Bugsy from the grass, "but I'm tired. I've got to rest."

"Well, I'm not going to let her get away with it. She'll kill you someday."

Maggie laid her net aside in the grass, got a firm hold on Pansy's bridle, and dragging the pony after her, searched the clearing until she found a strong, pliant switch. At the sight of the switch Pansy shivered and, as Maggie mounted, sighed plaintively, hung her head and stumbled forward like a pony who has been driven too hard and is about to give up the ghost. A cut of the switch and Pansy revived sufficiently to pick up her feet and trot. Maggie trotted her once around the clearing, then drove her at the wall. Pansy approached the wall at a cautious canter, lowered her head, and was absorbed in preparations for a repetition of her recent success when Maggie gave her a cut that made her change her mind and jump.

"See," scolded Maggie, "you can do it. You're just lazy," and she drove Pansy back and forth over the wall until the pony was jumping neatly, smoothly, and with a show, at least, of enthusiasm. Maggie patted her neck, dismounted, and handed her over to Bugsy.

"She won't try that again for a while."

"Thanks." Bugsy nodded and climbed aboard. "I think we ought to get those butterflies home before they hurt themselves. If they mate in captivity, we'll have hundreds of Mourning Cloaks and make hundreds of dollars."

Maggie whistled. "I forgot all about them. I hope mine is all right." She looked back at Star, still waiting obediently. "I'll jump Star over the wall," she decided,

32

"and we can go on through the woods and come out in the big field behind the house. It'll be quicker than going back to the road. You go ahead," she told Bugsy. "I'll be right along."

Maggie was relieved to find her butterfly still fluttering inside the net. She showed it to Star before she mounted.

"It's just an old butterfly net with a butterfly in it. Nothing to get excited about."

She mounted and walked Star up to the stone wall to look it over before they jumped. A moment later they were over and trotting after Pansy.

When the woods thinned out, Maggie came abreast of Pansy and Bugsy.

"Where do you think I'm going to keep those butterflies?" demanded Bugsy.

"Don't you have a cage or something?"

Bugsy shook his head and smiled a sly smile.

"I thought you had a cage ready. What are you going to do?"

"I'm going to keep them in Grandfather's study." Bugsy grinned.

"Just loose?"

He nodded. His eyes gleamed like marbles. "That's why it's such a good place. I've been thinking about it while I was riding along. It's always shut off. No one ever goes in there except maybe Miss Urquhart once a year to clean. I'll put in elm and willow branches, and put around saucers of sugar and water, and the Cloaks can fly around and eat and mate and lay eggs just as if

33

they were out in the woods. Better," he added, "because they won't have any natural enemies."

"What will Gran say?"

Bugsy looked prim. "She won't know."

"No, she probably won't," Maggie agreed, "but I just have a feeling that if she did know she wouldn't like having Grandfather's study turned into a butterfly farm."

"I have the same feeling," admitted Bugsy, "but if we're going into business, we've got to consider the butterflies first." He stared thoughtfully at Pansy's ears. "Anyway, even if Gran wouldn't like it now, if she knew about it, which she won't, she will like it when we start making money."

"I wish we could start making the money a little sooner," put in Maggie. "You didn't see Star jump that wall. She'd win that Junior Hunter Stake. I know she would."

"I'll do the best I can," replied Bugsy. "I'll try to borrow. With Grandfather's study all full of cocoons" — his eyes widened and widened and his mouth opened as the wonderful prospect took shape — "the cocoons will be security for the loan. Anyone would lend us money if they could see them there all over the study, ready to hatch." Bugsy's voice trailed off. He stared enraptured at Pansy's ears, seeing not them, but hundreds upon hundreds of little brown cocoons.

The horses trotted out from among the last trees into a field which had originally been cleared to provide a view from the back windows of Woodfield, the Armistead residence. It was a rambling, many-gabled building, half brick, half shingle, a comfortable and not very authentic adaptation of a Tudor manor house. It sprawled in all directions, with shabby outbuildings and an unkempt tennis court clustering about it.

"Haloo! Yoo hoo!" A remarkably strong alto voice, slightly cracked on the high notes, hailed the children from the back door.

"She's taking the scraps to the chickens." Bugsy roused from his reverie. "If I hurry I can get the butterflies all fixed up in the study before she gets back."

"Come on then," urged Maggie. "We'll gallop right across the field and round the house. Gran will love to watch us. She hardly ever gets a chance to see Star really going."

Maggie pressed Star to a canter. With a little more urging, the mare extended her pace to a full gallop. Pansy, still chastened, followed at a good clip. Halfway across the field, however, she began to lag. Bugsy, dreaming of cocoons, did nothing to prod her on, and Pansy lumbered more and more slowly.

"Ride that pony, Bugsy Armistead," shouted his grandmother. "Get after her. She's going to sleep. Use your legs. Use your crop. Kick her. Hit her. She's hardly moving."

The old lady punctuated her shouts with alternate swishes of her cane and her scrap bucket. Her voice rang out. Bugsy realized that he was not distinguishing himself before his grandmother. He belabored Pansy with his legs, but he couldn't beat her now with the net.

35

She ambled past the old lady and around the corner of the house.

"Shame on you. Never give in to a pony. Heels down, elbows in. Now hit her. Why don't you hit her?" The powerful alto cracked with annoyance.

Bugsy came to a stop in the drive at the front of the house.

"All you women think about is riding, riding" he exclaimed petulantly. "I'm not sure it's good for the butterflies to be jounced around so much."

Maggie was too exhilarated after her gallop to notice Bugsy's ill temper.

"You take the butterflies into the house and get them fixed up. I'll take Pansy down to the stable for you."

"Thanks." Bugsy dismounted, handed Pansy's reins to Maggie, and carefully holding the two nets ran under the porte-cochere, up the steps and in the front door of Woodfield.

# 4

Turning away from the house, Maggie with the two horses set off down the drive toward the stable. For almost a quarter of a mile the drive wound through fields enclosed and divided by white fences, all in need of paint. In the angle where the drive joined the State road stood the stable. Happily, Maggie thought back over Star's fine jumping and her gallop across the field. After seeing that, Gran must realize that Star was as good as the best horses they had ever had at Woodfield. She was as strong, fast, and fearless as Red Pepper, but gentle and easily taught. She was as clever as Ghost, or Fancy, or Amber, or Bluebell, or Arrow. As Maggie said over their names, the horses of the glorious past seemed to take shape and canter past carrying their gay, dashing riders: Gran on Arrow, Grandfather on the terrible Red Pepper, her father and mother on Ghost and Fancy, and Aunt Cinny, a girl then, on Bluebell. Of the riders, only Gran and Aunt Cinny were still alive. Of the horses, only Bell and Arrow remained at Woodfield. As if summoned by Maggie's thoughts, these two valetudinarians now hobbled to the fence to welcome Star and Pansy home. Arrow, a big brown gelding, had, in his prime, carried old Mrs. Armistead triumphantly over every fence and wall in every hunt within a fifty-mile radius of Woodfield. Bluebell, a gray mare, lame now, but still beautiful, had been to Cynthia Armistead what Stardust now was to Maggie. Cynthia, as she grew older, had schooled and hunted more highly bred and spirited horses, but Bell was the one she had always loved best. Indulgently, Maggie let Star and Pansy pause to exchange greetings with their elderly friends. As Bell stretched her neck over the fence and nodded her head in sage agreement with some remark of Stardust's, Maggie leaned down and hugged her horse's neck.

"You're just as smart as Bluebell, Star, and just as beautiful and fast and brave, and I'll always love you, and when you are old and stiff, you can graze all day in a nice green pasture, and I'll take just as good care of you as Aunt Cinny does of Bell. Even," she added wistfully, "if I can't afford it either."

Pansy, who had apparently been recounting her misfortunes, emitted a sigh so profound as to be almost a sob. Seeing her there plump, spotted, and overflowing with self-pity, Maggie was reminded of Sweet William, another spotted and emotional pony, who had flourished at Woodfield in the days of its greatness and whose exploits had become legendary. Maggie's father had ridden William to and from school from the first grade through the seventh. On the morning that William first saw his master set off on a large, strange horse, it was more than he could stand. He broke out of his stall and chased them, intent on some kind of revenge. A few minutes late he arrived at the boys' entrance to Wolverton Academy and penetrated halfway through the door before he stuck fast. It had required the combined efforts of Maggie's father (excused from class for the emergency), Gran, Michael, and Grandfather (hastily summoned by telephone) to dislodge William, who bit at one end and kicked at the other. Grandfather found it an outrage that Wolverton Academy hadn't a door wide enough to admit a Welsh pony. He said the place was a firetrap, and as soon as William had been extricated, Grandfather rode all over town until he found the chairman of the school committee and punched him in the nose. This made Grandfather feel better, and the next day he was sorry he'd made such a fuss and gave the town enough money to build Henry William Armistead High School.

In his declining years Sweet William was allowed to roam at large. One summer afternoon he had walked through an open french window into the drawing room where Gran was serving coffee to ladies. He had helped himself to all the sugar in the bowl, sampled the cakes and then, planting himself in the middle of the room, had endeavored to make light conversation. The ladies ran shrieking into a corner where they barricaded themselves behind an ottoman. Gran, to teach them not to be such idiots, received Sweet William like another guest. Ignoring the entreaties of the ladies, she chatted with William on subjects of mutual interest until he took his departure, again by the french window. The moment William's hind legs were outside, the ladies charged forth, upset the ottoman, banged the french window to and, turning on Gran, showered her with insults and abuse. First Gran laughed at them, but when they went on being rude, she told them that she found the conversation of an intelligent pony more interesting than all their silly chatter, and they could take a lesson in manners from William. He had been a perfect gentleman, but they had knocked over the furniture and cracked a pane of glass without even saying they were sorry, and now they were shouting like a bunch of loonies from the asylum. The ladies left and never came back, and a good thing too.

There were other stories of the old days. Maggie's father had bet his little sister, Cynthia, that she couldn't ride Red Pepper in a local point-to-point. Red Pepper was the fastest and best jumping horse in the hunt, but he had the hardest mouth and the worst temper. He dumped Cynthia three times before she got him in hand and rode him to win first place and a purse of one hundred dollars. Money, Maggie reflected, didn't matter in those days. They gave their cash winnings to the S.P.C.A. All that mattered was the horses. Gran had broken her hip because she wouldn't give up with a mean horse. It was a big bay that had been badly broken and badly treated, and Gran was trying to school it for a friend. The horse reared again and again, lost its balance and fell backward. Maggie could almost hear the thud and the shriek of pain as the horse went down. Michael had had to shoot it. Gran tried to throw herself clear, but her right hip was crushed, and she had been lame ever since. All this happened when Maggie was a little girl. She remembered Gran with her leg in a cast, and how Aunt Cinny had been too busy to take her out on the lead rein because she had to exercise all Gran's horses every day to keep Gran from worrying herself sick about them. Just last fall, Aunt Cinny's mare, Amber, the last of the Woodfield-trained hunters, had been sold to pay for the winter's supply of coal. Maggie sighed as she thought of how she wanted to buy back Amber for Aunt Cinny and how impossibly expensive it would be.

"Always walk your horse until it's cool. Never let it stand. If I've told you that once, I've told you a hundred times," growled a hoarse voice just beside Maggie.

She turned to find old Michael, the stableman, scowling up at her.

"I'm sorry. I forgot."

Michael grunted. "Where's Bugsy?"

"I left him at the house."

41

"How'd Pansy get her legs cut?"

For the first time Maggie noticed that Pansy's forelegs were bleeding. She explained about Bugsy and the stone wall.

"I hope I did the right thing," she said uncertainly.

Michael grunted again, and taking Pansy's reins led her to the stable. Bent, shriveled, and stiff in the joints, he hobbled in front of Maggie, muttering to himself. Maggie followed at a distance.

In the stable where the unused stalls far outnumbered the used, Maggie took off Star's saddle and bridle and left her at the water trough while she mixed an extra portion of grain for her supper. When Star finished drinking, Maggie brushed her coat, cleaned her hoofs, led her to her stall, and fetched the grain. For all his age, Michael's eye was sharp.

"That's too much oats," he growled from under Pansy's foreleg, which he was washing. "Do you want her to jump over the moon?"

"It's not too much. I'm going to work her hard all day tomorrow."

"Not tomorrow."

"Yes I am. It's Saturday." Maggie tossed her head.

"Can you forget?" With a creaking of joints, Michael reared up from beneath Pansy and pointed at Maggie with his sponge. "You who every day pass the beautiful monuments set there in the Family Plot to remind us of the departed. You, the blood descendant of those departed, can you forget them?"

42

"No," interrupted Maggie, "I remember now. I really do."

Michael flourished his sponge. His old eyes gleamed. "Who could forget what happened that day?" he demanded. "First we put in Mr. Wallace, wild Mr. Wallace that scoffed at sacred things and couldn't ride a horse, and came to a bad end." Michael heaved a loud and mournful sigh.

Maggie seized the moment. "I know. I remember. Tomorrow we clean up the Family Plot and on Sunday are the ceremonies." She nodded brightly at Michael, but it was no use. Michael was off. Deprived of most of his horses and all his stable hands, Michael found relief for loneliness in long, impassioned outpourings. Once started, he was as irrepressible as the Ancient Mariner, whom he also resembled in appearance. Maggie leaned against a post. The tale that Michael had to teach was one that Maggie knew well and could not choose but hear.

Ten years ago, Mr. Henry William Armistead, Maggie's grandfather, had decided to forgive his harum-scarum brother Wallace for living riotously, writing poetry, and dying ignominiously. He had his brother's body dug up from its pauper's grave in a western mining town and brought back to the Armistead family burying plot. There with appropriate ceremonies the bones of Wallace Armistead, whose reputation as a poet had grown in the five years since his death, were laid to rest beneath an appropriate monument. The ceremonies were attended by family friends, local dignitaries, and the representative of a leading New York newspaper, as well as by all the Armistead family except for Maggie and Bugsy, who were considered too young. Their poor foolish parents, scarcely older than children themselves, drove twenty miles from their own home in an evil contraption with the sinister name of Stutz Bearcat.

Maggie suppressed a yawn. Michael's eye glittered fiercely and he spake on.

By afternoon all the guests had left except for the newspaperman from New York. The Old Master, Mr. Armistead, had asked him to stay to read some letters written by Wallace Armistead. Something the newspaperman said must have set off the Old Master's temper, which was violent. He had thrown out the newspaperman and was still bellowing with rage when Madam came back to the house from the stable where she had been helping Michael with a sick horse. Madam was used to her husband's tantrums. She left him alone for a while to quiet down, but this tantrum was too much for the old man. It killed him.

"But Death hadn't done with us yet that day," Michael intoned with gloomy gusto, and he went on to relate the day's culminating tragedy.

Maggie's parents were summoned back by telephone. They had only just got home, but they jumped back into the Stutz Bearcat and set off again for Woodfield. At the level crossing at Wilmerstown they ran head on into the Montreal express, which was doing sixty on a down grade.

"And so," Michael concluded in a quiet, happier tone, "Madam had another monument erected in the Family Plot, and every year on the anniversary of the tragedy the Town of Wolverton holds a ceremony there to honor the memory of its richest citizen and all his relatives that lie near him."

Michael drew a deep, contented breath. The recitation had done him good. Maggie eyed a pile of gardening tools by the door.

"Will we have to work all day tomorrow?" she asked.

"We will work all day tomorrow," replied Michael with pride, "and we still won't satisfy Madam. She wants that Family Plot as neat and well tended as if there still were four gardeners here to do it."

Maggie nodded. She had thought so. She gave Star a frugal supper with a carrot for dessert, patted her, said good night to Michael, and started up the drive toward the house. The weekend which she had planned to devote to Star must be devoted instead to gardening and to tiresome memorial services for a grandfather and parents who, though once dear, were now, for Maggie, only the shadowiest of memories. There was no help for it. It meant a lot to Gran.

It was almost dark when Maggie climbed the steps to the front door. A light was burning in the foyer, and as she pushed open the massive door and entered, her grandmother came forward to meet her.

"That's a very pretty mare you have, Maggie," declared the old lady, "and you've done a fine job of schooling her. As she stretched into the gallop she reminded me of the little horse, Fancy, that I schooled for your mother. I don't want to raise your hopes too high, but I believe, Maggie, that if you keep at it, you'll get to have as much skill with horses as I had myself, or as your poor aunt had before she gave it all up." The old lady sighed, then nodded encouragingly at Maggie. "You're patient, and you have good hands, and, after all, you are my granddaughter." Old Mrs. Armistead smiled and threw back her head. Though she was old and lame and clad in an apron and house dress, she still had the fine presence of a Thoroughbred.

"Oh Gran!" exclaimed Maggie.

Such praise drove away all her troubles and disappointments. She ran to the old lady and hugged her.

"I was afraid you'd be late." The old lady patted Maggie's black hair. "We must eat dinner right away." Her voice fell to a confidential whisper. "I've made soufflé. It's in the oven."

Suddenly Maggie was hungrier than she had ever been. She sniffed the air, and mingled with the dank smell of the foyer, she thought she detected the fragrance of chocolate.

"Oh Gran!" she exclaimed again.

She gave the old lady another hug and bounded into the washroom at the back of the foyer to get ready for dinner.

Mrs. Armistead limped to the foot of the vast stair-

46

case, drew a deep breath, and boomed into the upper darkness, "Cynthia, dinner."

"Coming," replied a faint, faraway voice.

"Bugsy!" The old lady boomed again.

There was a faint scuffling in the drawing room or perhaps in the corridor which connected it with the closed-off study. Startled, Mrs. Armistead peered here and there into the shadows. A moment later, Bugsy popped up, as if by magic, at the foot of the staircase.

"Here I am." He smiled a broad, disarming smile. The old lady gave him a sharp look, then shrugged.

"Hurry and wash. I've made a surprise for dinner. It's in the oven."

"Yum," cried Bugsy, and he too made for the washroom.

# 5

Oᴌᴅ Mʀs. Aʀᴍɪsᴛᴇᴀᴅ turned off the light — to save electricity — and threaded her way through the dark dining room to the butler's pantry, where the copper sink and the glass doors of the china cabinets gleamed softly in a beam of light from the open kitchen door. Here she paused to survey the kitchen, once the domain of a cook and numerous helpers, but now her very own. Three springer spaniels dozing around the vast and shining black cookstove acknowledged the presence of their mistress with tail wags, then dozed off again.

On the top of the stove a stewpot and a teakettle simmered. From the stove's interior came soft snapping sounds, while through the cracks around the lids and the chinks in the drafts the fire gleamed red. A great copper boiler, polished to a mellow glow, loomed at one side, and up from the back of the stove reared an intricate superstructure of shelves, cubbyholes, and warming ovens bedecked with iron garlands and embossed with nickel knobs. An oval table spread with a checked cloth and set for four occupied the center of a wide expanse of floor. Along the wall opposite the stove stretched the soapstone sink. Oiled and rubbed to a sheen, it provided a rich background for the tracery of copper pipes that twined all over it to blossom in two enormous faucets. The far walls and corners with doors leading to pantry, cold room, laundry, and back stairs lay in shadow except here and there where the red glow escaping from the crevices in the stove cast dancing lines and squares and rectangles of light.

Mrs. Armistead's nostrils dilated as she tested the progress of her cookery. With a satisfied nod, she shut the pantry door on outer chill and darkness and made her way between the spaniels to the stove. Again the spaniels wagged but made no effort to get out of her way.

In the shadows the door to the back stairs was pushed open, and Cynthia Armistead stepped into the room. She carried a sheaf of papers in her hand, and after closing the door behind her, she walked to the center of the room and paused under the light to study them.

With her free hand she tugged thoughtfully at her short golden hair. Mrs. Armistead turned from stirring the stew.

"Aha, there you are."

Cynthia looked up, drew a deep breath and smiled.

"It smells wonderful." She put down her papers by the sink. "What is it? Did you shoot it or did you steal it?" Cynthia's voice was softer than her mother's, and her face, which was pretty rather than handsome, lighted up with a gentle, diffident humor when she smiled.

"Both wrong." Mrs. Armistead emitted a delighted chuckle. "I charged it."

Still smiling, Cynthia shook her head. "It must be your manner even more than your name. The tradesmen are like the horses. They respond to you. The cooks who used to cook for us never cooked half so well as you do, Mother. What is the other smell that is so delicious but isn't stew?"

"That, my dear," replied the delighted old lady, "is the chocolate soufflé. I think you are right about the cooks."

Old Mrs. Armistead removed the plates from one of the warming ovens and dished out the stew, while Cynthia carried the plates to the table. Maggie and Bugsy bounced in and greeted their aunt so enthusiastically that they almost knocked a plate of stew out of her hands into the waiting jaws of the spaniels, who had bestirred themselves and were following Cynthia back and forth between the table and the stove. When everyone was seated, the spaniels closed in on Mrs. Armistead. They rested their heads on her lap, and with mournful eyes watched each mouthful she took. Saliva flowed in strings from their jaws. At intervals one or another emitted a gluttonous yelp.

"This is wonderful, Mother," said Cynthia.

"Ummm," mumbled Bugsy.

"And I'm starved," declared Maggie with her mouth full.

Cynthia shook her head at Maggie's manners, but old Mrs. Armistead beamed on them all and surreptitiously fed a piece of meat to a spaniel. This set off a fracas which threatened for a moment to upset the table. Mrs. Armistead clouted all the spaniels and restored peace. She looked somewhat sheepishly at her daughter, then with a defiant toss of the head she took two more pieces of meat from her plate and fed them to the spaniels who had missed out on the first round.

"They're hungry," she said.

Two worried lines appeared in Cynthia's forehead.

"So am I." Still chewing, Maggie held out her empty plate. "More?"

"There's plenty more," said Mrs. Armistead. "Just help yourself from the pot."

In a single sweep Maggie rose, shoved back her chair, and lunged, plate in hand, at the stove.

"Just a minute. Please finish what you are chewing and wipe your mouth before you ask for more, and then say 'Please.' You don't have to chase after your food as if you were afraid someone else would get it first. There's plenty for everyone." Cynthia's gentle voice rose. "Just because we eat in the kitchen doesn't mean that we have to behave like — like — spaniels." Her gray eyes, usually so mild, moved sternly from Maggie to her mother.

Maggie stopped short. Her cheeks flushed. Old Mrs. Armistead folded her hands and stared down at her plate. Looking at them, Cynthia leaned back in her chair and began to laugh.

"I'm sorry to be so cross at such a delicious dinner. Help yourself, Maggie, and give us all some more, but be a little more gentle about it. I've been doing accounts," she explained. "They always make me cross, and I've been talking to Mr. Purinton on the telephone."

"He'd make anyone cross," declared Mrs. Armistead, eager to make amends. "When your father was alive to tell him what to do, he was all right, but left to himself —" The old lady wrinkled her nose in disgust.

"Don't be so hard on him," said Cynthia. "A lot of other men besides Mr. Purinton who were supposed to know all about investments gave bad advice and didn't foresee the crash in 1929. We aren't the only ones who lost a fortune."

Bugsy, who had been eating quietly and efficiently, suddenly raised his hand for silence.

"The way to lick this depression is by spending," he announced. "We must grease the wheels of industry, and the way to do that" — he paused and scowled — "oh yes," he remembered, "the way to do that is for

52

Aunt Cinny to turn in the Pierce-Arrow for a new Chrysler, and Mr. Crosby will give her a good deal even though the Pierce-Arrow is —" Bugsy strained to remember until his eyes protruded. He shook his head. "I can't remember the word."

"If it's young George Crosby who told you all this," said old Mrs. Armistead, "forget it. His father is a fine man and knows horses, but young George is a robber. Always has been."

"Does he mean he'll give me a new Chrysler in exchange for the Pierce-Arrow?" asked Cynthia.

Bugsy thought hard. "No, I'm sure he doesn't mean that."

"And where does he suggest I get the money to pay for the new Chrysler?"

"You borrow it," replied Bugsy, "and that greases the wheels of —"

"Bah," exclaimed Mrs. Armistead, "that's George all right. Up to his old tricks."

"I'm afraid you're right," said Cynthia.

"He told me to tell you," said Bugsy, "and I did. Please put a dumpling in mine." He held out his plate to Maggie, who was dishing out the stew.

When everyone was served, Maggie sat down carefully at her place and with a real effort to be ladylike asked, "What did Mr. Purinton say on the telephone?"

"I'm glad you asked me" — her aunt nodded at her — "because I think I'm not going to follow his advice this time, and you'll all have to take the consequences."

"Good for you," put in Mrs. Armistead.

"I wish I were sure." The two lines reappeared in Cynthia's forehead. "Mr. Purinton wants me to sell some stock to take care of our expenses. I'll only get about one fourth of what it cost Father when he bought it. It's a chemical company that makes synthetic materials. I can tell you quite a lot about the company. I've been studying about it."

"Don't, dear," said her mother. "These things always take so long, and we wouldn't understand a word."

"I won't try to explain then, but I do think the company is sound and that if we hold on to the stock, it will begin to regain its value fairly soon."

"Good," declared Mrs. Armistead. "Hold on to it. He's a fool."

Cynthia raised her eyebrows. "The question is, how long can we go on living on the income we do have without some extra cash? I've been making calculations, and I think that if we are careful, we can get along another six months without selling anything." She looked from one solemn face to the other and tugged thoughtfully at her hair. "If we have to have cash in six months, we'll sell the stock, but meanwhile do you think you can get along without any extras, none at all?"

Maggie caught her breath. "No allowance?"

"Don't look so frightened, Maggie. I've counted yours and Bugsy's allowances as necessities. If you've been saving, you should have enough money by June to enter Star in something at the show."

"Oh I have been saving, Aunt Cinny, and I've got almost enough, but" — Maggie paused diffidently — "I

54

was counting on your paying me a dollar to paint fences. Is that extra?"

"No, I guess not," smiled Cynthia, "especially since we already have the paint."

Maggie leaned back and sighed in relief.

"I know you'd like to enter Star in the Junior Hunter Stake," Cynthia went on seriously, "but I really think that such a young horse with no show experience and very little jumping experience hasn't much chance. She's sure to get excited. She won't do her best. She might even hurt herself. It's not worth risking eight dollars that we don't have."

"Oh Aunt Cinny, you haven't seen her lately. I've been schooling her every day. She's quieted down, and she loves to jump. You ought to see her."

As soon as Stardust entered the conversation, Mrs. Armistead's interest kindled.

"She's right, Cynthia. Maggie has a very promising mare. Of course, you can't be sure how she'll behave in a crowd of strange horses, but as far as conformation and movement go, she's very promising."

"If you can earn the money, Maggie, then go ahead. I wish I could pay your entry fee for you, but —" Cynthia shrugged and shook her head.

Bugsy's eyes had been bulging with pent-up information. He stood up in his place.

"Aunt Cynthia," he began.

"Don't interrupt, young man." His grandmother turned on him. "I must say I wasn't proud of you sitting like a sack of potatoes on that pony and letting her

55

do exactly as she pleased with you. Your Great-uncle Wallace never learned to ride, but I didn't think a grandson of mine would let a pony get the better of him. Now you know perfectly well —"

Bugsy squared his shoulders, bit his lip, and bravely rode out his grandmother's lecture on horsemanship. When she finished, he again fixed his aunt with earnest eyes.

"You can be sure I'll never ask for extra money because I've started a business which already brings me a small income." He cleared his throat modestly. "In six months I'll be able to help you. So don't worry. Maggie's in the business too. Sort of."

"Of course I'm in it."

"That's wonderful, Bugsy," said Cynthia. "What is the business?"

"I think I'd better not say just yet. I'm just beginning, and I think I — I mean we — should keep it a secret. You'll be surprised." He couldn't repress a giggle.

"There, you see," exclaimed Mrs. Armistead. "He's like all the Armisteads. He has hidden abilities. You don't notice them right away, but when they're needed they come out. It's the same with Cynthia. When we need a financial wizard, she turns out to be one. It's the same with me. When we need a cook, I turn out to be one, even though I'd never so much as toasted —" She clapped her hand over her mouth and jumped up. "The soufflé!" she cried. With a swipe of her cane she scattered the spaniels. In a moment she was opening the oven door.

The soufflé was a little black around the edges but delicious still, especially when covered with thick cream. The cream, Mrs. Armistead hastened to explain, was a present from their neighbor, Mr. Roote, to whom she had given advice about a sick horse. It hadn't cost a cent. They ate in silence while the spaniels, who had crept in close again, drooled on the floor, and the cookstove, emitting cozy snaps and pops, enveloped them in its warmth. Bugsy sucked the last crumbs from his spoon and leaned back.

"I like being poor," he said. "I like eating in the kitchen."

Maggie had taken possession of the soufflé dish and was scraping at it with a spoon.

"I never got to do this when we ate in the dining room," she murmured.

"You shouldn't do it here either," said her aunt, "but never mind. Enjoy yourself while you can. Sooner or later my financial wizardry will restore our fortunes, and you'll have to go back to the dining room."

Maggie laughed and scraped away harder than ever.

"Your aunt is absolutely right," said Mrs. Armistead, "but I was about to say something else." She bent her head for a minute. "This is hard to say, but tonight, as we were sitting here so comfortably just before the tenth anniversary, I knew I wanted to say it." She paused again in thought. "As for going back to the dining room, Cynthia, I like it better here. I'm growing old. Day after tomorrow ten years will have gone by since my husband, my son, and his wife all died in one day. Then I didn't care what became of me. I rode vicious horses because I hoped one of them would kill me. You know what happened." She lifted her cane and shook it for them all to see. "It served me right." She brought the cane down with a thump, unfortunately on part of a spaniel. The spaniel uttered a howl and crawled yelping across the kitchen floor.

"Great heavens!" cried the old lady and made after the spaniel. "Poor Adam." She bent to stroke his head. "Poor fellow." She felt him over with a practiced hand. Adam rolled onto his back, his tail quivered, and he bared his teeth in a sheepish grin. "He's not hurt." Mrs. Armistead patted him briskly. "He was just startled. Probably was having a dream. Sometimes he has bad dreams. Don't you, poor old fellow? Did you dream that someone kicked you? He used to get kicked pretty often when he was young and hunted with Henry. Henry thought he was scatterbrained. I think he still remembers bad things that happened long ago and has dreams about them." She returned to her place at the table. "As I was saying, I remember bad things too." She paused.

Very expertly, with a peristaltic motion, Bugsy had been working himself down his chair. The top of his head was just sinking below the tablecloth when his grandmother noticed him.

"Bugsy Armistead, you come right back up and stay

until I've finished. You children don't have any manners at all. Maybe we shouldn't eat in the kitchen,
Cynthia, after all. I'm sure I don't know. What I'm
trying to say is that I remember bad things too, but I
remember them without bitterness. Gradually, over the
last years since we've been poor, I've begun to enjoy
each day again. I don't feel like a cripple. I'm too busy,
and, I flatter myself, too useful. I may be too lame to
get to the stable very often, but I can look after my hens
and my dogs and my vegetables, and I can cook and wash
dishes and keep a clean kitchen." She glanced with
satisfaction over the big comfortable room. "Cynthia
will restore the Armistead fortune because she has in-
herited her father's business ability." The old lady
smiled affectionately at her daughter. "You've always
been so quiet and gentle, my dear. I never dreamed you
had Henry's financial sense."

"I haven't, Mother. Really I haven't. I may lose what
little we have left before I'm through."

"If you do, it doesn't matter. I'd rather be poor and
feel reconciled and forgiving. It took me a long time
to forgive your Uncle Wallace. He made nothing but
trouble when he was alive. When he was dead, and I
thought he couldn't make any more trouble, he seemed
to rise out of his grave to deliver the last and worst
blow of all."

"Oh no," Cynthia said. "You didn't think that!"

"Yes I did, but, thank heaven, I've got over it. Poor
Wally, who couldn't overcome his fear of horses enough
to get on one when he was alive, wasn't likely to rise

up out of his grave to bring about three deaths. No, no. I can see now that it was just chance, and that Wally was just unfortunate. I've taken up one of the old cabbage roses (they're going to rack and ruin in the garden now anyway) to plant by his monument. He was fond of cabbage roses. The most annoying thing about Wally was that he always gave me the feeling that when he said one thing he meant something else and was laughing at me all the time." Mrs. Armistead paused and added, "When he talked about the roses though, and how much he liked them, he was different, and I think he meant what he said."

"He really was fond of cabbage roses," said Cynthia.

"I don't see how you can be so sure. You never knew him. I did, and I was never sure of anything with him. I always had the feeling that he was — what's that expression you use, Maggie? It means to make fun of a person when he doesn't know it."

Maggie, who was putting Star through her paces at the horse show, stared blankly at her grandmother.

"Pulling your leg?" suggested Bugsy.

"That's exactly it," replied the old lady.

"We'd say he was fresh too," added Bugsy, inspired by success.

"You'd be right. He was fresh too." The old lady nodded. "I don't mind any more. I've forgiven him. He did make funny jokes. Once I laughed so hard at something Wally said that I fell right off the horse I was exercising. Even Henry thought his jokes were funny sometimes, but not often."

# 6

Softly, almost to herself, Cynthia said, "He never forgot the cabbage roses. They grew by the back door of the farmhouse when he was a little boy."

"That's right," exclaimed Mrs. Armistead. "I often played around the rosebushes with Henry and Wally when I was a little girl and my mother was paying a call on old Mrs. Armistead. We made mud pies and we decorated them with the petals. The bushes were still there after the farmhouse burned down and the family moved away, and I transplanted them here when Henry and I built this house. Henry thought they were untidy, but I liked them, and so did Wally." The old lady turned to her daughter. "How do you know so much about the roses, Cynthia? Wally never told you. He went West for good when you were a year old."

"He didn't tell me," replied Cynthia, "but he wrote about the roses in a poem. It was one of the last ones he wrote when he knew he was going to die. He meant what he said. He wasn't pulling anyone's leg."

"My dear Cynthia" — Mrs. Armistead's eyebrows rose in consternation — "you surely don't read Wally's poems?"

Cynthia lowered her head to hide a smile. "Yes, I read them over and over. There aren't very many."

"Oh dear!" Mrs. Armistead bit her lip. "I only read one, once. It was in a magazine, and it was called 'Horsey of Woodfield.' Naturally I thought it would be about a horse, but it wasn't. It wasn't really about anything as far as I could see, and it made me uncomfortable. Like a fool, I showed it to Henry. He flew into one of his rages and sued the magazine. He'd have sued Wally too, if he could have been found, but Wally was up in the mountains somewhere, prospecting." She turned on Cynthia. "You see, Wally always made trouble."

"Did you feel as if he was pulling your leg again?" asked Bugsy.

"Yes," replied his grandmother, "that's exactly how I felt. I never read any more of his poems. I didn't think anyone else did either."

"As a matter of fact," said Cynthia, "quite a few people do."

"I can't think why."

"I think they read his poems," said Cynthia slowly, "for the same reason I do. He says clearly and beautifully all the confused and complicated things that I and lots of other people feel but don't know how to say. Some of his poems are about being unwanted and inadequate and frightened. Everyone feels that way sometimes, but especially now with the depression, people have been shaken out of their secure beliefs and they feel more uncertain than ever. Perhaps that is why Uncle Wallace is so popular just now." Cynthia realized that her mother's face was puckered in distress. "What's the matter?" she asked.

"Poor child," Mrs. Armistead sighed. "You miss Amber, and you don't get out enough."

"No, no!" Cynthia's voice rose impatiently. She paused, tugged hard at her hair, and went on quietly again. "Of course I miss Amber, but that's not why I read Uncle Wallace's poems. I read them because I like them. I feel that Uncle Wallace understands me."

"I don't see how. You couldn't be more different. He did all sorts of wild things when he was off by himself, and he was afraid of horses, wouldn't learn to ride." Mrs. Armistead shook her head.

"Was Horsey of Woodfield a horse or a person?" asked Bugsy.

Cythia started and turned on him. "Have you been reading those poems?"

"Of course not," said Bugsy. "I've just been looking at Maggie. She's practically a horse, even though she's supposed to be a girl."

Maggie was posting to the left diagonal at Wolverton Horse Show, while, at the same time, she was making it difficult for herself by mouthing her bit, tossing her head, and skittering from side to side. Cynthia laughed. Mrs. Armistead gave a delighted snort.

"I was just the same at her age."

"What's the matter?" Maggie returned to reality, her suspicions aroused. "What's so funny?"

"You are," giggled Bugsy. "Horsey."

"Shut up!" Maggie leaped to her feet and started around the table after Bugsy. She stumbled over a spaniel and fell on the floor. The spaniel gave a howl, jumped up, rolled its eyes, staggered to the stove, and collapsed with all four feet sticking straight in the air.

Maggie got up. "There's no place to walk in this kitchen," she growled. "Gran's stupid old spaniels take up all the floor."

Mrs. Armistead hastened to comfort the injured spaniel. "Poor Flip. Poor girl. She didn't mean it."

Ashamed of her ill temper, Maggie also apologized. "I'm sorry, Flip, but really you do spread out an awful lot."

Flip's tail quivered. She heaved a sigh, rolled onto her side, and closed her eyes.

"Aunt Cinny," declared Maggie, "I don't see why you let Bugsy be so fresh. He acts like a big, spoiled baby."

Bugsy made a face at her across the table, and Maggie rose again in wrath.

"Stop it," said Cynthia, "and sit down. I'm afraid you are both spoiled babies. Bugsy tries to be smart, and you, Maggie, can't seem to put your mind on anything but horses. Do you know what we have just been saying about your Great-uncle Wallace?"

"No."

"He was a famous poet."

"Oh." Maggie registered polite surprise.

"Come, Cynthia," pleaded old Mrs. Armistead, "you are exaggerating."

Cynthia reached in the pocket of her skirt and drew out a wad of paper which, when unfolded, turned out to be a page torn from a magazine. She smoothed out the folds.

"This is a review of a book called *Wallace Armistead, The American Keats,* by Frederick Blinco," she said and began to read aloud.

"We happy few who read Armistead's poems as they appeared between 1900 and 1918 in magazines, and were first to thrill to his strange jazz-like rhythms, his brilliant imagery, his wit, and his melancholy cannot but be grateful to Mr. Blinco for his scholarly biography. The growing group of younger Armistead enthusiasts should also be grateful to Mr. Blinco for organizing and presenting an account of the career of their hero.

"However, it is unfortunate that Armistead, probably the most perverse and brilliant genius of his generation, should be first presented to society under such dull sponsorship as Mr. Blinco's. Blinco plods through the events of Armistead's short, breathless life, conscientiously separating fact from apocrypha in a welter of well-meaning footnotes. He then grinds out a conventional essay on the poems, the sort of thing an intelligent high school student could do better, decides that Armistead was like Keats in more ways than he wasn't, and ends on a note of self-congratulation at having made such a nice, easy book out of a poet of whom he hasn't the foggiest comprehension. One of those beautiful horses that cavort so decoratively through Armistead's imagery would, in the opinion of this reviewer, be better qualified than Mr. Blinco to write the biography of Wild Wally Armistead."

"Bah!" Mrs. Armistead brought down her fist on the table.

"It's almost the end," said Cynthia. "Let me finish." She read on:

"Now let me state some hard facts. Mr. Blinco's book is not all it should be, but it is the only full-length book on Armistead. Why is it that not one of the brilliant and gifted men who were his friends during his lifetime has written a book about him? There are reasons, to be sure. It is difficult to arrive at truths about a man who spoke of himself only indirectly in imagery often personal and perverse. There are very few poems, fewer letters, and no diaries to throw light on the workings of the poet's mind, and, of course, there has always been the hope that new, illuminating material would turn up. Ten years ago, at the death of Henry Armistead, the poet's elder brother, it was hoped that some family papers might be made available, but the Armistead family, whose members were never sympathetic to Wallace and had as little as possible to do with him, maintains that there are no documents pertaining to the poet in their possession. It seems unlikely that any new material will come to light. This disposes of the only valid excuse the friends of the poet have for not getting busy. Another book, of a very different ilk from Mr. Blinco's, must be written if Armistead is to be raised to the position among our great literary figures that is his by right!"

"That's the end," said Cynthia, "and it's signed with initials P.H."

"Those two writing fellows are in for trouble." Mrs. Armistead shook her head wisely. "Just as sure as they meddle with Wally, they're in for trouble. They have it already," she exclaimed, not without satisfaction.

"You can't tell me that Blinco is going to take that sort of thing from P.H."

"Is Great-uncle Wallace the one who couldn't ride?" asked Maggie.

"That's right," replied her grandmother. "I offered to teach him myself, but he wouldn't let me. He couldn't seem to overcome his fear."

"If you had listened to the review," said Cynthia a trifle sharply, "you would realize that the important thing about your Great-uncle Wallace was that he wrote good poetry. If you could take your mind off your horse long enough, it would do you no harm to read some of his poetry. You might even enjoy it."

Maggie made a face.

"Your aunt is right, Maggie," said Mrs. Armistead unexpectedly. "I know how you feel about your horse because I was just the same at your age, but you should try to think about other things like" — the old lady frowned — "those things you have in school, you know — arithmetic and history and Latin — and you should think about the state of the world, and what's the matter with the country, and you should read books, all sorts of books, even poetry." The old lady paused and bent her head. Seizing the ear of a handy spaniel, she scratched it as she went on. "When I was growing up, and we lived on the farm (it's Mr. Roote's farm now), I never read books or thought about anything but horses." She scratched harder at the spaniel's ear and kept her eyes lowered as if she was embarrassed to have

68

to make such a confession. "If I'd studied more at school and read more books, I might have known better what to do. I might have understood Wally better, and Henry too. Everything might have been different." The hind end of the spaniel wriggled while the front end gurgled in ecstasy. "Good Flounce," murmured Mrs. Armistead. "Good girl."

Cynthia leaned toward her mother as if to reassure her, but Bugsy spoke before she had a chance.

"I bet Miss Urquhart gave you that page of magazine."

Cynthia turned to him. "How did you know?"

"She gives me the same sort of rumpled-up pages out of magazines with things about insects on them. Every night she reads over the paper she collects out of the wastebaskets where she's been cleaning, and she picks out the things her friends will be interested in and gives them to them."

"I think she has a nerve reading everything she finds in our wastebaskets and giving them to other people she thinks will be interested," declared Mrs. Armistead.

"She only gives away printed things." Bugsy hastened to the defense of Miss Urquhart. "She doesn't give away written things because she doesn't think it's honorable."

"No," exclaimed Mrs. Armistead, "she just reads them herself."

"Not all of them," Bugsy explained. "She doesn't have time. Most of them she files away in her study because she's educating herself and when she doesn't have to work any more she can read all these things that she's —"

"Study indeed!" Mrs. Armistead exploded. "Really Cynthia, I don't see why we go on having her. She's an expense, and she's batty, quite apart from reading everything in our wastebaskets. You and I could do the cleaning as well as she does in half the time."

"I know we could," Cynthia sighed, "but I can't fire her now. She's worked for us in one way or another for over twenty years, and she has only a few other places left, and they're not very regular, and she's poor and old and queer." Cynthia frowned. "It's like Michael," she added. "Maggie and I could do what he does, but what would become of him?"

"Of course," replied Mrs. Armistead. "Of course you're right, and if there's any stew left, you might take it down to Michael when you go to check on the stable."

Cynthia stood up. "I'll put the stew in his pot. Have you anything else for him?"

The old lady stood up too. "I've put some cookies aside from the batch I made for Sunday." With her cane she made a path between the spaniels and disappeared into the pantry.

"I'll come with you," volunteered Maggie.

"No," replied her aunt. "You help Gran with the dishes. Bugsy?" She eyed him curiously. He was leaning back in his chair with his eyes closed. "Bugsy?"

He gave no sign of consciousness. His breathing was

70

deep and regular. Cynthia smiled and winked at Maggie.

"It's too bad he's asleep. I was going to ask if he'd like to come with me and hold the flashlight and look for moths."

"Sure I'll come. Give it to me!" Bugsy sprang to his feet.

"No sir," replied his aunt. "One trick deserves another. You help with the dishes, and then you are both to go right to bed."

Taking a pot of stew, a packet of cookies, and a flashlight, Cynthia disappeared out the back door.

"Michael," she reported on her return, "is enjoying his supper. He's warmed up the stew on his stove, and he's made a cup of tea to have with the cookies. I was late, and I don't think the poor fellow had anything to eat there at all. We must remember to bring him something every night, even though he is supposed to look after himself. It's begun to rain, but he says tomorrow will be fair. He can tell by the way his second left rib throbs where Red Pepper kicked him in 1900. He has sharpened the tools and packed them in the Pierce-Arrow ready for tomorrow. That is the report from the stable."

Cynthia put the flashlight away and hung the old coat she had been wearing in front of the stove to dry. "Now, Mother, you go up to bed. You've worked all day and cooked us a wonderful dinner, and you need a good rest before tomorrow. I'll empty the ashes and

71

bank the fire and put the dogs to bed and tend to the lights and the doors."

Mrs. Armistead stowed away her dishpan and wiped out the sink.

"If you don't mind, I will go right to bed. I'm suddenly quite tired." The children and Cynthia kissed the old lady good night and, leaning on her cane, she climbed the back stairs to her room. Cynthia took up the papers she had been studying before supper and sat down with them at the kitchen table.

"Now Bugsy and Maggie, you get to bed. If we do everything in the Family Plot that Gran wants done tomorrow, we're going to have to work hard all day."

The children kissed their aunt good night and, in response to beckonings and head jerkings, Maggie followed Bugsy through the butler's pantry and the dining room into the dark foyer. After the kitchen it was miserably damp and chill.

"What is it?" asked Maggie. "I'm cold. I want to go to bed."

Bugsy took her hand. "Just come and see how I've fixed up the library for the butterflies."

He led her through the drawing room, down the corridor, and pushed open the massive door of Grandfather's library. As he felt around for the light switch, a stale odor of dust and disuse drifted into the corridor. Bugsy found the switch and, like a scene on the stage, the room leaped from the darkness. It was a large room, paneled in walnut and lined with rows of books expensively bound. Above the fireplace, opposite the

72

door, the portrait of a fierce gentleman in a frock coat glared with protuberant eyes at whoever entered. The furniture was massive and modern, except for an ancient grandfather clock with a list and a dirty face which stood to one side of the fireplace. Its spidery hands pointed to six fifty-eight, and in the little archway above the face a painting of greenish fruit hung askew. Through the long glass panel set in the pendulum case, the brass pendulum could be seen hanging motionless and plumb, but at a disconcerting angle to the listing case. It was a homely, farmhouse sort of clock, and it backed awkwardly against the wall like a country cousin among fashionable relatives. It was even dustier than anything else in the room, although under the electric light a coating of dust showed on the desk and the tables.

As soon as her eyes were accustomed to the glare, Maggie searched for Bugsy's arrangements. "I don't see anything," she said.

"That's good. I hoped you wouldn't. I didn't want it to show from the door in case Gran or Aunt Cinny should look in. Look!" Bugsy pointed to half a dozen saucers unobtrusively scattered on the tables and floor. "Some of them have sugar and water in them, and some of them have dog meat. I remembered that butterflies love carrion so I took a little dog meat out of the kitchen when Gran wasn't looking. Then I cut branches of trees and put them in pails of water so they'll sprout leaves for the caterpillars to eat. They're pretty well hidden behind the furniture."

"It's wonderful," said Maggie, "but be sure to warn Miss Urquhart before she cleans or she'll throw everything out. I guess she does clean sometimes," she added thoughtfully. "The clock is a lot dustier than anything else."

"I'm going to," replied Bugsy. "She'll understand."

"Come on," said Maggie. "I'm tired, and it's cold here, and I don't like the closed-up smell, and that portrait of Grandfather, and that dirty old clock that no one's touched since he . . ." She shuddered. "They give me the creeps. Come on."

"I hope they'll be happy and propagate," said Bugsy.

He switched off the light and closed the door gently. They returned to the foyer, mounted the massive staircase, and threaded their way down long corridors back to the kitchen wing where, to save heat, the family now occupied the small servants' bedrooms.

# 7

AT NINE O'CLOCK the next morning, with its body
gleaming in the sunshine and its motor purring sedately,
the Pierce-Arrow banked into the final curve of the
driveway and rolled to a stop under the porte-cochere.
Cynthia, who was driving, lowered her eyes from the
windshield to the array of levers and pedals which
sprouted from the dashboard and the floor. Her
knuckles showed white as she gripped the wheel. She
ground her lower lip between her teeth and studied her
feet. Suddenly and with determination she lifted her

left foot off the clutch pedal and at the same time poked the brake with her right foot. The Pierce-Arrow jumped straight up in the air, shot forward, jumped again, trembled all over and stalled. Cynthia stamped wildly on brake, clutch, and floor boards, while she made futile grabs at the emergency brake and the gear stick. When the car stopped trembling and stood quite still, she dropped her hands to her sides, leaned back, and shut her eyes.

"Oh dear," she moaned, "I mixed them up again."

Michael, who sat beside her and had been hauling back on the reins for all he was worth, rolled his eyes, muttered an incoherent prayer, and collapsed into himself until he looked like a heap of old rags on the shiny leather seat.

From the steps where she stood leaning on her cane and balancing a box of pansy plants in her free hand, old Mrs. Armistead had shouted useful instructions throughout the crisis.

"Get hold of her. Turn her. She's got an iron mouth. Use your curb. That's what it's for."

Maggie and Bugsy stood beside their grandmother and supported between them a large old-fashioned cabbage-rose bush. The roots, along with a generous hunk of native soil, were wrapped up in a piece of burlap, and the children with their arms under the hunk of soil were pretty well incapacitated. They just stared through the rose stems until the Pierce-Arrow came to rest several yards beyond the porte-cochere. At this point Mrs. Armistead commanded,

"Come on quick before she tries to back."

Five minutes later, Mrs. Armistead and the children were installed in the tonneau along with a lawn mower, two grass rakes, a spade, a shovel, an edge cutter, a sickle, a saw, a pair of clippers, a large basket of well-rotted horse manure for the shrubs, and two pails filled with an assortment of seed packets, nails, screws, bolts, and carpenter's tools. Mrs. Armistead still held the basket of pansies. Michael and Cynthia shared the front seat with a pail of chicken droppings for the grass, and the rosebush. A hole had been torn in the burlap when the bush was installed, and native soil began to dribble out onto the floor of the Pierce-Arrow. Like the boy at the dike, Michael plugged the leak with his finger.

"Left, clutch. Right, brake," murmured Cynthia. She peered into the mirror, in which she could see that some kind of struggle was going on between Bugsy and Maggie. "Please be quiet," she begged, "while I start."

"Be quiet," trumpeted Mrs. Armistead. "No, you can't go back for your net. Sit still, both of you. Don't startle her. Do you want her to bolt?" The struggling ceased.

Once more Cynthia gripped the wheel and took stock of the levers and pedals. She pressed the self-starter and the motor purred. Very carefully she shifted into low gear. Holding her breath, she released the clutch and gently pressed the accelerator. Michael braced his legs, but the Pierce-Arrow gathered itself together with scarcely a jerk and began to roll. Majestically it proceeded down the drive and turned off onto a narrow, surfaced road which ran between neglected pastures. This was, in fact, a continuation of the road along which Bugsy and Maggie had ridden from school until they abandoned it for the butterflies and cut home through the woods.

In the early eighteenth century, when the first Henry William Armistead built his farmhouse beside it, this road had been the only one between Boston and the village of Wolverton. In the mid-nineteenth century it had fallen out of general use when a new road was built giving access to the railway line. After the old Armistead homestead burned in 1885, and the family moved away, the road was almost completely swallowed up in woodland. Meanwhile, with the coming of motorcars, the new road was macadamized and became the State road. Not until Grandfather Armistead made a fortune and decided, in 1902, to build a mansion near the site of his family farm was the old road rescued and revived. For most of its length, it was used only as a bridle path, but on the section which ran between his new mansion and the old Armistead family burying ground, Grandfather Armistead had expended both cash and foresight.

"Your grandfather," remarked Mrs. Armistead as the Pierce-Arrow wove its stately way between the frost heaves and potholes which now marred the road's hard surface, "foresaw the motor-propelled hearse, but Cynthia, if it's possible when I die, will you try, dear, to get a hearse drawn by — I'm sorry, dear, I forgot you were driving."

"Was that the field where you had the jumps for train-

78

ing the hunters?" asked Maggie, pointing to an expanse of alders.

"I think so." Mrs. Armistead peered out the window. "You'd never know it now, with all that brush. We had three or four fences, a bank and a stream, then we crossed the road, went down another bank and over two stone walls that were left in the old cellar hole. That last part was very tricky."

"There's the cellar hole now," said Maggie, "and I'm going to try Star on the bank and the stone walls. I'm sure she can do them."

"Don't be rash," advised Mrs. Armistead. "Don't let her overdo. Aha!" She craned forward. "There's the monument. I think it's very handsome. I know Henry would have liked it. I'm not so sure about your dear mother and father, Maggie. They were very dashing and modern. They used to laugh at our old-fashioned taste. Well, well, I did the best I could."

The Pierce-Arrow rounded another curve, and straight ahead, from the middle of the Family Plot, the monument soared into the pale blue sky. It was a granite shaft, thirty feet high. On the top crouched a veiled mourning figure in polished black marble. Old Michael looked up and, as the black marble shot forth shafts of reflected sunlight, his watery old eyes lighted and shot forth an answering gleam. Forgetting the leak, he lifted his hands in a gesture of reverence.

"How splendid," exclaimed Mrs. Armistead. "It quite dwarfs Wally's angels, and that, after all, is how it should be."

"I like the angels better," announced Bugsy. "That black thing on top makes me sad."

"It is sad," replied his grandmother. "Sometimes I still —" She paused, and for a moment bowed her head. "But Wally couldn't help it. He'd been dead five years." She drew a deep breath. "I'm glad you like the angels," she said to Bugsy. "Your grandfather picked them. He thought they were what Wally needed to keep him straight in the hereafter. And now Wally is famous. Well, well." She gave a little chuckle.

The angels, five in all, clustered around the base of a broken pillar of white marble. It was only half as tall as the shaft to Henry William Armistead and his son and daughter-in-law, but with all the angels it was obviously expensive, and the white marble was very showy. The slate headstones of earlier, humbler generations of Armisteads huddled together in a corner. Some leaned against the iron rails of the fence for support, some leaned against each other, and others clustered timidly around a huge lilac bush which stood in their midst like a shaggy old watchdog. When, as the Pierce-Arrow drew closer, one of the headstones seemed to sway back and forth, Mrs. Armistead's eye was caught and drawn away from the monuments.

"What's going on?" she asked. "I thought I saw Great-aunt Jane Tyler moving."

"She's walking," said Maggie.

"Impossible," replied her grandmother. "She weighed two hundred and eighty. Didn't take a step for twenty years." The old lady stopped short and caught her breath. "Good heavens, Cynthia, there's a live man in there with the old Armisteads."

The Pierce-Arrow bucked and swerved, but Cynthia got hold of it again.

"I see him," she whispered through clenched teeth.

He emerged from behind Great-aunt Jane Tyler's headstone and walked slowly across the plot toward the gate. He was a tall young man wearing knickerbockers and a sweater. He had no hat, and his dark hair was clipped short.

"Who can that be?" demanded Mrs. Armistead.

As if in reply to her question, the man turned and looked full at the approaching car. His face, though still young, was pale and drawn. His eyes showed as dark hollows.

"I think I've seen him somewhere," continued Mrs. Armistead.

Cynthia gave a cry. The Pierce-Arrow swerved and lunged straight at the ditch. With a thud the massive radiator head buried itself in the dirt. The front mudguards, where the headlights sprouted like lilies, hit and crumpled. There was a tinkling of shattered glass. The motor choked and died, and with a shudder the great shining limousine sank to rest. Only, high in the air, the back wheels still revolved.

# 8

THE YOUNG MAN reached the car a few moments after the accident. With difficulty, because, besides being nose down, the car had settled with a list, he opened the right front door. Michael and the rosebush slid out. The young man caught them, but they were followed so quickly by the basket of chicken droppings and Cynthia Armistead that the young man fell back, stumbled, and all three landed in the ditch under a shower of chicken droppings.

"Cynthia," began the young man. "Miss Armistead."

Over Michael and through the rosebush Cynthia stared at him.

"I saw you. I knew it was you, and I —" She buried her face in her hands.

The young man jumped to his feet just as Michael, with a creak and a groan, rose up in front of him. He clenched his gnarled fist and shook it at the Pierce-Arrow.

"Damnation to you and to all the infernal combustion engines that come roaring out of Hell to carry us to death. It was one of you that did in young Mr. and Mrs. Henry, and today you tried to get the rest of us. Go back where you came from. Damnation to you all!" Michael made a terrible sound in his throat, and his old eyes glowed with fury. Then his knees gave way. He sat down in the ditch beside the rosebush and again plugged the leak with his finger.

"Cyn — Miss Armistead, are you hurt?" The young man bent over her.

Cynthia shook her head and wiped her eyes. "I'm all right, but please see about the others. They're in the back." She pointed with a shaking hand. "I'll look after Michael."

The young man had to jump to reach the door handle. When the door swung open, he swung with it, which was fortunate for him because the lawn mower hurtled out and would certainly have felled him if he had been in its way. The head of Bugsy, with eyes like doorknobs, appeared shortly after the passage of the lawn mower. He slid forward slowly, holding himself back with his feet until the young man could reach his hands and swing him down. Cynthia, who had soothed Michael and left him to rest in the ditch, came up in time to put her arms around Bugsy.

"Are you all right? Are the others all right?"

"I'm all right. Gran poked me in the stomach with her cane and Maggie landed in the manure basket. What happened?"

Cynthia ran to the car door. "Mother, Maggie, are you hurt?"

"We are quite all right." Mrs. Armistead's voice boomed firm and clear from inside the car.

Maggie peered over the sill. Like Bugsy she slid forward on her stomach until the young man could swing her to the ground. Along with her came a heavy fall of manure. She shook herself, and more manure came off. Mrs. Armistead now appeared on all fours in the open door. She had smears on her face, and her pug was askew.

"My dear, I'm so glad you're not hurt. How is Michael?"

"He's shaken up, but I don't think he's hurt."

"Then we are all safe. Thank heavens for that." Mrs. Armistead considered the distance between herself and the ground. "How am I to get down?" she asked, then nodded at the young man. "How do you do?"

"Very well, thank you." He stepped forward. "If you will allow me, Mrs. Armistead, I'll swing you down as I did the children."

"You are very kind." Mrs. Armistead nodded again,

but drew back. "I knew the moment I saw you that we had met before, but your name escapes me. I'm quite old you know, and my memory isn't at all what it should be. Did you ever hunt with the Wolverton Pack?"

"No. Never." The young man looked alarmed, then collected himself. "My name is Martin Drew. We met ten years ago. Now, if you will place your hands on the running board and lower your shoulders —"

"Yes, of course." The old lady observed Martin Drew with a puzzled but friendly eye and disregarded his invitation to place her hands on the running board and lower her shoulders. "You were a friend of my son perhaps, my son Henry, who was killed." She smiled apologetically. "He had so many friends that sometimes I forget."

"I'm sorry, Mrs. Armistead." Martin shook his head. "I knew your son only slightly. I had just met him when —" He stopped abruptly, then held out his arms. "Please, ma'am, let me swing you down. You must be uncomfortable crouching up there."

"You are very kind, but I'm quite comfortable, and you see" — she shook her head and smiled again — "I broke my hip some years ago, and I'm a little afraid of being swung. It's foolish of me, and if it is the only way down, I shall of course swing, but I'll need my cane when I land." She gave a slight shudder, set her mouth in a determined line, reached the cane out of the tonneau, and handed it down to Martin.

"Please pardon me," begged Martin Drew. "I never thought. It was most inconsiderate of me. I didn't know, and you see I remember you as so very tough. I mean —" His pale face turned beet red.

Mrs. Armistead, however, was not at all offended. "I *am* tough," she replied proudly. "I have always been tough, and if there is no other way down, I'll swing." She gripped the running board and began to wriggle slowly forward. Martin watched her with admiration. Suddenly he raised his hand.

"No," he cried. "There is a better way. If you will wait for five or ten minutes, I think I have a better way to get you down." He smiled up at her.

"I don't mind waiting," she replied and returned to her original crouching position with evident relief.

Still holding Mrs. Armistead's cane, Martin Drew dashed to the road, turned left and sprinted down it in the direction of Wolverton.

"Of course," exclaimed Mrs. Armistead, "I remember him now. He doesn't look healthy, otherwise I'd have remembered him at once. Well, I hope he comes back. He's taken my cane with him." She settled into a more comfortable crouch. "He was very pleasant when he stayed with us, wasn't he, Cynthia? I seem to remember that you liked him and that your father liked him before he got so angry and threw him out. He was terribly angry." The old lady shook her head. "I can still see him raging around the foyer, waving Wally's letters and shouting terrible things about him. I said, 'Henry, I'm going to wash my hands, and then, if you'll try to control yourself, I'll listen to you.' He shook the letters at me and shouted something about how he'd like to throw out the letters and every last trace of Wally just the way he'd thrown out that conceited young puppy. I went into the washroom, and while I was drying my hands, I heard him winding his old grandfather clock that had belonged to his mother and that he set such store by. I felt pretty sure that if he puttered with the clock (you know how he loved it and never let anyone else wind it or touch it, and no one has to this day) he would gradually quiet down. I went into the kitchen to talk to the cook. When I came back, Henry was lying across the threshold of his library."

Mrs. Armistead sighed and backed into the interior of the tonneau. There, unseen, she could be heard blowing her nose. In a few minutes she reappeared.

"We've had a slight accident," she declared, "the sort of thing you have to expect with motorcars. It's no excuse for dawdling. Here." She began passing down garden tools more quickly than her relatives could catch them. "Michael!" Michael jerked to attention.

"Take a shovel and plant that rosebush. It goes just to the left at the front of Mr. Wallace's monument. Bugsy! Fetch water from the brook for the rosebush. Maggie, I've rescued most of the pansies. Get them in right away. Make a border around the big monument. Cynthia, you start raking, and when you've cleared the beds, you can put in the seeds, and there's the grass to be raked and cut and the edges to be straightened. We can't afford to dawdle."

While she gave orders, Mrs. Armistead continued to hand down tools. "There," she said at last. "Now get to work, all of you. Don't worry about me, Cynthia. I shall crouch here until he comes, and he won't come any faster because you keep looking for him." Mrs. Armistead beat an impatient tattoo on the doorsill and with a determined toss of the head tore her own eyes from the track through the woods and fixed them on the Family Plot.

The others took up their tools, stepped over the railing, and under the eagle eye of the old lady set diligently to work. For five minutes all was hard work and quiet. At last, so faint as to be almost indistinguishable from the scratching of Cynthia's rake, a series of little pops jarred the quiet. Mrs. Armistead cocked an ear. The pops became louder and louder until a sustained grinding arose deep and low, swelled until it smothered the pops, and finally burst with a detonation that shook the landscape. As the explosion reverberated into silence, the pops began again, sharp now as rifle shots, and out of the woods bounced a shiny black Model T Ford sedan. Its little engine hood was jiggling with the exertions of the motor within. It had lost its radiator cap, and a geyser of boiling water spouted at regular intervals, fell hissing on the radiator, and rose again in puffs of steam. As the front wheels hit the improved road, the back wheels kicked out and the exhaust exploded again, emitting smoke and fire and a lusty bang. Bouncing now out of sheer exuberance, for the improved road was quite flat, the little car tore along popping like a rifle match, until Martin Drew, who sat at the wheel of this spirited contraption, cut the motor. The regular swish, and sizzle of the geyser as it went up and came down became audible along with subterranean gurglings and hissings within the radiator. The little car rolled in under the up-ended stern of the Pierce-Arrow and slid down its starboard side so close that its roof brushed the Pierce-Arrow's running board, and Mrs. Armistead drew back. With a screech of brakes, Martin Drew brought the Model T to a halt and jumped out.

"I knew she could do it," he cried. "It was a close thing, but she didn't fail me. At one grade we had to turn around and go up backwards. In some places I just left the road and blazed a new trail through the wilderness." He grinned up at Mrs. Armistead. "I'll bet this is the very first motorcar to come all the way through from Wolverton on the old road. Oh Emmy, Emmy, my great big beautiful baby, how I love you." He blew a kiss at the little car, and in reply its radiator bubbled affectionately.

From her perch Mrs. Armistead took in the situation and approved. "Mr. Drew, you are very ingenious. I understand what I am to do." She disappeared inside the Pierce-Arrow and emerged again feet first. While she was placing her feet on the roof of the Ford, Martin couldn't help but notice that her sneakers had large holes in the soles.

"Now," said Mrs. Armistead when she stood on the roof of the Ford, "I shall lower myself to a sitting position with my legs hanging over the edge. My feet will reach down to the radiator hood. Please, Mr. Drew, may I have my cane?"

With apologies, Martin took the cane from the interior of Emmy and handed it to her.

"You are doing exactly right," he said, "and if you will give me your hand, you will find it's an easy step from the hood to the fender, then to the running board, and from there to the ground. Don't be afraid that Emmy will cave in when you step on her because she won't. She's very strong."

Mrs. Armistead took Martin Drew's proffered hand, and a moment later she was standing on the ground. First she brushed the manure from the shoulders of her jacket and shook out her skirt, then, hooking the cane around her neck, she gave a twist to her falling pug and nailed it in place with a hairpin. Finally, having unhooked the cane with her left hand, she seized Martin's right hand in her own and shook it vigorously.

"Thank you very much," she said. "If you hadn't had that good idea, I don't know how I'd have got down because, quite frankly, Mr. Drew, I'm not at all sure I'd survive swinging." Martin Drew mumbled modestly, and the old lady continued. "I am very glad that we've met again. Ever since my husband's death I have felt that I owed you an apology." Martin mumbled again, somewhat incredulously. "Yes, I have," she assured him. "My husband had a terrible temper, Mr. Drew, but he was always sorry afterwards. I don't know what you said or did to anger him, but I do know that if he had lived, he'd have been sorry that he sent you off so rudely. Actually he liked and admired you. I should have written you all this, and I would have if I hadn't

90

been overwhelmed by so many distressing events." She nodded toward the Family Plot. "You heard about my son and his wife?"

"Yes," replied Martin. "It was a great calamity, a loss to society as well as to their friends and family."

Mrs. Armistead sighed, then jerked herself together and gave Martin's hand a final pump. "Well, well, that's that. Now, if you will excuse me, I'll get to work. We must have the place cleaned up and ready for the memorial ceremonies tomorrow. My husband, you know, did a great deal for the town of Wolverton. The civic authorities hold a memorial service here each year on the anniversary of his death. This is the tenth and rather special. I expect you came to report it for that newspaper of yours." She smiled hopefully.

"As a matter of fact, that wasn't why I came." Martin Drew looked the old lady straight in the eye. "I came here to consult with you and Miss Armistead on a matter of business concerning the poet, Wallace Armistead."

"Oh." Mrs. Armistead frowned. "He crops up all the time. Cynthia is the expert on business and on Wallace Armistead too. She's going to be busy gardening all today, and tomorrow we have to get the house in order for the reception after the ceremonies. I don't believe she can discuss business before Monday afternoon. We wash in the morning." Mrs. Armistead gave Martin Drew a nod of dismissal and turned her attention to a trellis which stood very much askew at the main entrance to the Family Plot.

Martin Drew was not discouraged. "There's no great hurry. I can see her at any time that is convenient for her. As a matter of fact I'm on a sort of vacation. That's why I came here through the woods instead of coming properly up to the house. I remembered the old road because Miss Armistead took me on a walk along it when I was here before. It was such a pleasant walk. I've always remembered it. Today I took Emmy as far as she could go easily and then walked on."

"You'd have found it even pleasanter on horseback," remarked Mrs. Armistead, still studying the trellis. Scowling, she marched up to it and shook it.

Left alone, Martin turned and realized that the Pierce-Arrow was still firmly embedded in the ditch. To haul it out would require something more high-powered than Emmy. A trifle timidly he followed the old lady.

"Perhaps," he suggested, "I should drive to your house to tell the people there about the accident. With a good truck, or," he added hastily, "a pair of strong horses and a man, we could get your car out."

"You are very kind," replied Mrs. Armistead, "but there's no one at the house and we don't have draft horses or a truck." She shook the trellis again and it collapsed at her feet. She stared down at it and sighed.

Martin Drew glanced quickly at the workers in the Family Plot. Cynthia's elbows stuck out through holes in her sweater as she raked, and Maggie, on hands and knees, displayed to full advantage the patch on the seat of her Colonel Roosevelt breeches. Martin Drew frowned thoughtfully, then shrugged his shoulders and addressed the old lady again.

"Let me help you fix that trellis. I'm quite good at repairing things."

Mrs. Armistead's face lighted. All formality and brusqueness left her. "You really are kind," she smiled. "We're none of us good at carpentering, and I'd hate to have the mayor and the rest of them march in through this broken-down old trellis. If you can fix it, I'll be very grateful."

# 9

FOR THE REST of the morning, under Mrs. Armistead's direction, everyone worked his hardest. As soon as Martin Drew had repaired the trellis, he was given a saw and pruning shears and told to prune out the wild grape vine which had crawled in from outside and got itself thoroughly mixed up in the ancient lilac bush. Hacking and sawing, Martin forced his way into the center of the tangle. The sweat poured down his face. At intervals he had to sit down to catch his breath and rest his arms, and he noted with grudging admiration that Mrs. Armistead, Cynthia, and even the creaking Michael had twice his stamina.

At noon, Mrs. Armistead called a recess. Martin offered to drive everyone back to the house in Emmy. With the adults inside and the children swinging from the running boards, Emmy bounded over the hardtop, nimbly dodging the holes and heaves. She drew up, brakes shrieking, under the porte-cochere. Mrs. Armistead extricated herself from the front seat as fast as she could, then, as if to show that for all her distrust of motorcars in general she felt only gratitude to Emmy and her master, she invited Martin to lunch.

"It won't be the way it used to be," she told him. "I'm the cook now. The food is plain, but good. Better, if you ask me, than when I paid a cook to spoil it. You look tired, and I'm sure you are hungry. You must stay."

She took the children with her to help in the kitchen. Cynthia was left in charge of Martin Drew. After he had washed up, she ushered him somewhat timidly into the drawing room and asked him to wait while she helped Michael at the stable. Martin had no sooner sunk into one of the enormous overstuffed armchairs than he fell fast asleep.

He awoke with a start to the awareness of something rummaging around the room. As his eyes focused, he saw that Cynthia, on hands and knees, was peering, then reaching under a sofa. She drew out a bone, added it to a little pile of bones in the center of the carpet, and crawled on to the next chair. From under it she drew, in addition to a bone, a sneaker and a rubber ball. Still too drowsy to feel surprise, but with a limp, detached interest, Martin watched Cynthia make the rounds of the furniture and add considerably to her pile. She sat back on her heels, pushed her short hair back from her face, and sighed. Then she dropped her head and buried it in her hands. Martin, awake now, and with a flush of embarrassment because he was watching her at a moment when she believed herself to be unobserved, shuffled his feet and sat up.

"It was rude of me, but I fell asleep. I hope I haven't slept too long."

Cynthia jerked up her head. "No, no; only about half an hour. Lunch isn't ready yet." She smiled at him.

"You see," he explained, "I've just got over pneumonia. I must seem very feeble to you."

"Oh dear," she jumped to her feet, "I'm sorry. I thought you looked pale, but I didn't know why. I hope you won't get sick again from working too hard. You should have told us."

"No, no," replied Martin, "I like working. Exercise and fresh air are what I need, but your mother sets quite a pace."

"Yes, it means a lot to her to have everything in order for tomorrow."

"Does it mean a lot to you too?"

"Oh yes, I can't let her down. We have to keep up appearances. Otherwise we become objects of pity, and we couldn't either of us stand that. If I keep working, I can get everything done. That's why I'm picking up bones now. I'll clean tomorrow. You see, the mayor and all the rest of them come here for refreshments after the ceremony." She studied the shabby, dusty

96

room, sank suddenly to her knees and retrieved another bone from under a corner of the rug. "It's the dogs," she explained. "They bury them here because no one comes in much, and they don't like to go out in cold weather. I don't believe poor Miss Urquhart has cleaned here since — Oh well." She stood up and approached Martin. "May I ask your advice about something?"

Martin straightened in his chair and gave her his sympathetic attention.

"Do you think," she asked, nervously rubbing her hands together, "that I could sell the Pierce-Arrow for enough money to buy a Ford like yours?"

"My dear girl," exclaimed Martin, "you should be able to buy three or four Fords like mine for the price of that Pierce-Arrow."

Cynthia shook her head. "I should," she said, "but I won't. I've got to sell the Pierce-Arrow through George Crosby because there's no one else. First I've got to hire him to pull it out of the ditch, and he'll charge just as much as he dares for that. There's no one else to do it, and he knows it." Sitting down near Martin, she went on to explain that George wanted the Pierce-Arrow for a tow truck, but that he also wanted to sell her a new Chrysler. George's character being what it was, she felt that when she refused to be tempted by the new Chrysler, he would offer a ridiculously low price for the Pierce-Arrow. "How much," she asked, "is a reasonable price?"

Martin rather enjoyed being asked for advice. He

considered the matter. "I think you should be able to get about two hundred dollars for that Pierce-Arrow, if it isn't too badly damaged." He rubbed his chin. "For two hundred you should be able to get a very good, small, used car that would be cheaper and easier to run than the big limousine."

"I know I'm not a very good driver," Cynthia interrupted, "but I think I would do better with a smaller car."

"You didn't do well this morning, I must admit." Martin smiled at her and shook his head. "You steered her right into the ditch."

"That," broke in Cynthia, "was different. I mean it wasn't because of my driving. It was because I was looking —" She bit her lip and blushed. "It was because I wasn't looking at the road," she finished lamely.

"Well, well." Her humility quite touched Martin. "You telephone this Crosby to come and haul the car out of the ditch. Make him name his price before you hire him. When he's got the Pierce-Arrow out, you tell him you might be willing to sell it to him for four hundred dollars as a special favor because you know he wants it. When he objects to that, I'll take over."

"Thank you. Thank you very much." Cynthia smiled. "I try to be a good business woman, but with someone like George, I know I'm licked before I even start."

Maggie bounced in.

"Lunch is ready, and Gran's made an omelet so you've got to come right away before it falls. Oh, there's my sneaker. I've been looking for it all winter."

"Here, Maggie," said Cynthia, "take some bones too. No, Mr. Drew, you don't need to take any. They're quite disgusting, really." She began to pick them up.

"I don't mind them," said Martin as he helped her, "and you used to call me Martin. I wish you would again."

"Yes, I did. I didn't think you remembered." Cynthia looked up at him, then hastily lowered her eyes. "It seemed quite natural then. Now, I don't know."

By the end of lunch, Martin had been accepted as a friend of the family, and both Cynthia and her mother were finding it quite natural to call him by his first name. Mrs. Armistead took a motherly interest in his health. She had once had a horse that died of pneumonia in spite of everything she could do to save it. She realized the seriousness of the disease, and she made Martin promise that as soon as he had driven them back to the Family Plot, he would lie down in Emmy, wrap himself in a blanket, and rest until George Crosby arrived. She looked forward immensely to the discomfiture of George.

"Have another peach, Martin," she urged. "I put them up myself. They are very wholesome. Maggie, pass the cookies to Martin. He needs to eat to build up his strength if he is to outsmart George."

The spaniels, wagging their stub tails and slavering, caught whatever came their way and waited, ever hopeful, for more. Martin ate ravenously.

"I don't know when I've had such good food, or when

I've been so hungry. Yes, thank you, I will have more."

The luncheon was broken up by the appearance of Michael at the back door. He was ready to go back to work. The sight of him — aged, bent, and conscientious, with his hat in his hand and a whetstone under his arm — made everyone leap from the table. Cynthia ran to telephone for George Crosby and his truck. Mrs. Armistead and the children hastily cleared the table and stacked the dishes.

# IO

THE AFTERNOON was far advanced when George **Crosby**
stopped his tow truck under the stern of the Pierce-
Arrow. Inside the Family Plot, Mrs. Armistead, Cynthia,
and Michael were putting the finishing touches to the
grass. In the field, Maggie and Bugsy were burning
brush. Emmy lay concealed behind a clump of bushes
at the edge of the woods. Curled up in her back seat,
Martin had again fallen asleep. George Crosby climbed
out of the cab of his truck and made a careful inspection
of the Pierce-Arrow.

"Hello there," he called to Cynthia as she came out
to the road to meet him. "Not much left of the old bus,

is there?" He clicked his tongue and shook his head. "It's headed for the right place all right. You just picked the wrong graveyard. Ha, ha. Now" — he rubbed his chin — "the problem is to get it to the right graveyard, the junk yard. Ha, ha, ha."

"No," replied Cynthia with spirit, "that's not the problem. The problem is to get it out of the ditch so that I can drive it home."

Once more, but with an expression of infinite sadness, George Crosby shook his head and clicked his tongue.

"If you think you're going to drive this pile again, you're in for a terrible disappointment. I hate to tell you this, but this ain't a car any more, it's junk. The whole front end is shot, the wiring is gone, the radiator's cracked, the steering mechanism —"

"Let's get it on the road first," insisted Cynthia, "and then we'll see about the damage."

"O.K." George shrugged. "The customer is always right."

Cynthia stood to one side while George maneuvered his tow truck into position. She glanced toward the clump of bushes, but although the truck made loud noises, nothing stirred. When the Pierce-Arrow's rear end was satisfactorily chained to the winch on his truck, George, maneuvering carefully and with great skill, hauled the big limousine out of the ditch and onto the road where it stood muddy, disheveled, with its headlights hanging as if in shame. George jumped from his cab.

"Now just let me show you about this front end.

Uh huh." He shook his head dismally. "It's even worse than I thought."

"It looks all right to me," retorted Cynthia. Again she glanced toward the bushes and was heartened to see old Mrs. Armistead disappearing behind them. "I'll just get in and start it," she said briskly. "It's a wonderful old car. They don't make them so well any more."

As she was about to step into the driver's seat, George leaped in front of her and barred the way.

"Don't try to start that car, Miss Armistead. Don't try it."

"Why not?"

"Why not?" George rolled his eyes. "Because when you step on that self-starter the chances are ten to one she'll blow up in your face. Boom!" George waved his arms and made a hideous face.

Cynthia jumped back, and for just a second a smile flickered in the corners of George's mouth.

"Now, Miss Armistead" — both his face and voice expressed deep concern — "I think I know your problem, and I want to help you. What you need is a good, practical, small car, and I've got just the thing."

Desperately, prayerfully, Cynthia turned again toward the bushes. To her unspeakable joy, a resounding bang shook the stillness. A string of poppings followed, and Emmy bounded into view. She tore straight at the group in the road, then with her characteristic screech, she stopped short. Martin leaped out.

"Is this the Pierce-Arrow that's for sale?"

Startled in spite of herself, Cynthia retreated to the

side of the road. "No," she said. "I mean yes."

Martin heaved an enormous sigh of relief. "Thank heavens. I'd have hated to come all this way on that road and found someone else had got ahead of me." He pulled out a handkerchief and wiped his face.

George Crosby's eyes widened. He took a cautious step toward Martin. "Did you drive here along that old cart track?" He nodded at the woods.

"Cart track is right," exclaimed Martin. "You sure hit the nail on the head that time, mister. What's the matter with people around here anyway? Can't they keep their roads any better than that, or do they still drive round in buggies?"

"You'd be surprised," replied George, "how backward some folks is around here."

Martin surveyed George and appeared to find him sympathetic. He winked at him. "I can see you're right on the ball." He gave a friendly nod. "I guess you don't let much grass grow under your feet as some do."

"I try to keep hustling," replied George, not displeased by the compliment.

"That's the only way to get ahead these days," said Martin. "Times are bad. Granted. O.K., but if you've got a little something here" — he tapped his forehead and gave George another friendly nod — "and if you don't mind hustling, there's still a living to be made in this old country."

George grinned. "That's just like I try to tell them round here, but they're so stuck in the mud they're like they was dead." He gestured at Emmy's New York plates. "In the big city, I guess things is different."

"Yeah, that's right." Suddenly abstracted, Martin was looking at his watch. "I got a terrible schedule," he explained. "When you work for Uncle Sam, you can't lie down on the job. Now lady" — he bore down on Cynthia — "you own this Pierce?"

"Yes."

"You wanna sell it?"

"I might."

"You might?" Martin sighed and turned to George. "Where I come from either you want to do something or you don't." George nodded his sympathy. "Come on now, lady," Martin went on with a great show of patience, "make up your mind. Do you, or don't you?" Cynthia looked in his eyes for a sign, but they remained hard. "How much did my friend here offer you?" he demanded.

"I ain't made no offers," said George smoothly. "All I'm interested in is fixing this young lady up with a nice new Chrysler 50 that goes."

"Say you'll accept four hundred," whispered Martin.

Cynthia stepped boldly up to George. "I'm not anxious to sell the Pierce, but for four hundred dollars I might let it go."

George clapped his hand to his forehead, staggered, and went through all the customary gestures indicative of stupefaction. Martin meanwhile made a quick inspection of the Pierce.

"Mind if I start her up?" he asked Cynthia.

"No, but be careful. It may —"

Martin was already in the driver's seat adjusting the formidable row of buttons on the dashboard. A minute later the Pierce broke into its low, steady purr. Martin cocked his head and listened. George Crosby, apparently forgetting the danger, came close and bent his ear over the hood. He lifted the hood and looked inside. Martin climbed out of the car and joined George under the hood. They emerged together. Martin reached inside the car and turned off the ignition.

"Well," he asked George, "how much do you want to offer for it? You got here first."

George rubbed his chin. "I'm not saying I couldn't use this car myself in business, but what I really want is to fix the young lady up with a good new Chrysler that runs. Now, if she wants to turn this Pierce in on a new Chrysler —"

"No," said Cynthia firmly, "I don't want a new Chrysler."

"Listen, Miss Armistead, you just let me bring one round and give you a spin in it. You'll change your mind."

"Look here," Martin interrupted, "I'm working for Uncle Sam, and, like I said, I got a tight schedule. I can't wait around while you sell the lady a Chrysler."

"What I don't see" — George's eyes narrowed, and he spat his words with a viciousness that belied his recent hearty manner — "is how you found out about this Pierce anyway?"

Apparently oblivious of George's suspicions, Martin slapped him on the back. "You don't miss any tricks," he chuckled. "I'll tell you. The government's got agents all over." He lowered his voice confidentially. "I can't tell you too much, but I'll tell you this. Before he's through, Uncle Sam's going to own all the old Pierces in the country."

"Yeah? What's he gonna do with them?" George's eyes widened again.

"Who knows?" Martin shrugged. "Maybe they'll just rot in a warehouse. The way they got things in Washington now with this New Deal, nobody knows what they're doing or why, but we're all keeping active because if you don't hustle, you're out."

George nodded and thrust his head close to Martin's. "How high you willing to go?" he whispered.

Martin laughed. "You're a pretty smart cookie. I like you, and I'll help you all I can, but there's some things I can't do."

Solemnly now, George turned back to Cynthia. "You're making a mistake not to look into the Chrysler, but for old time's sake, Miss Armistead, I'm willing to offer you fifty dollars for this heap. That's forty dollars cash after I've deducted the towing charge." George gazed sadly at the Pierce, shook his head, rolled his eyes piously, and went on: "That's a fair, square offer, and I don't mind telling you, it's more than I ought to pay."

"No," replied Cynthia. "No."

Again Martin chuckled and slapped George's shoulder. "You're all right," he said. "You figure to get your money back doubled or tripled from the Uncle, and you're right too." He winked. "But I can't let it go without a struggle. I got to keep the interests of my employer in mind." He turned to Cynthia. "One hundred dollars, and the Uncle pays the gentleman for towing."

"No, I'm asking four hundred dollars."

"Everyone's out to get what they can from Uncle Sam," Martin sighed. "You got to expect it. After all, that's what they think he's for." Martin shook his head accusingly at Cynthia. "Lady, you can't be that mean to your old Uncle, not so long as he's still got a few honest guys like me working for him. One hundred and fifty, and that's the limit."

"A hundred and seventy-five," said George.

Martin paced up and down rubbing his forehead. "Two hundred," he said.

"Two hundred and twenty-five," said George.

Martin opened his mouth.

"And forget the towing charge," added George quickly.

Martin winked ever so slightly at Cynthia, then he shook his head at George. "You win. I can't go higher. Not right now."

George fixed Cynthia with narrowed eyes. "O.K., Miss Armistead. That's my offer. What do you say?"

Cynthia heaved a long sigh. "I guess I might."

"Might, guess, maybe, perhaps!" Martin poked George in the ribs. "Women," he whispered. "Write her a check now, before she changes her mind. I can't promise, but I got a pretty good idea Uncle Sam will be back. You can't lose."

"Would my personal check for two hundred and twenty-five dollars help you make up your mind?" George whipped a checkbook from his pocket and flourished it under Cynthia's nose.

She hesitated, then said sadly, "You are too smart for me, George. I can't resist cash. Give me the check, and the dear old Pierce is yours."

Martin watched closely while George wrote his check. When it was safe in Cynthia's pocket, he seized George's hand and pumped it. "So long, George. I'm awful glad to have made your acquaintance, and don't think I bear you any grudges, because I'm not that kind. I've got to be moving, but you may be hearing from us again. Good luck. Goodbye, ma'am." He bowed to Cynthia. "Can I get back to a main road without going over that buggy route again?" Cynthia directed him. He looked at his watch. "Holy cats! I got to hustle!" He leaped into Emmy and was off in a barrage of pops.

George left soon after, dragging the Pierce behind him. He was in a happy mood, and his last words as he leaned from the cab of his truck were an urgent invitation to Cynthia to drop in and look over that new Chrysler any time, just any time.

Mrs. Armistead emerged from the bushes shaking with laughter.

"I haven't enjoyed a show so much since the last time your father took me to hear Sir Harry Lauder." She collapsed by the side of the ditch with a whoop of delight. "There's a clever young man, and, Cynthia, for someone who always got stage fright in school plays,

109

you acted like a trooper. Of course," she added, "if I hadn't gone and waked Martin up, he'd have slept right through. Come, children," she shouted, "come and hear how your aunt and Martin made a monkey out of George Crosby. Ha, ha."

The children, who had long since burned their brush, but were under strict orders to stay out of the way until called, galloped up to look at George Crosby's check and hear their grandmother describe the brilliant performance of Cynthia and Martin. Old Michael, stiff though he was, managed with a terrible creaking of joints to slap his thigh several times, while emitting a prolonged guffaw. When, a short time later, Martin himself returned in Emmy, he was hailed as a hero, showered with praise by Mrs. Armistead, begged by the children to act it all out again, and more quietly, but just as sincerely, thanked by Cynthia.

"If you hadn't come, I'd have given him the Pierce in return for towing it away."

Flushed with pleasure, Martin said, "It was fun, wasn't it?"

For some minutes both he and Cynthia were overcome with laughter.

Emmy, a truly remarkable vehicle, proved able to carry all the tools as well as all the people. She just had to do it in low gear. Once again with a screech of brakes, she deposited the Armisteads under their porte-cochere, and once again Mrs. Armistead extended an invitation to Martin.

Could he come to dinner with them on Monday

evening at half-past six? She couldn't ask him tonight because there was nothing in the house fit for him to eat, but she would go at once and kill the two young roosters so they could hang until Monday. Then, stuffed and roasted, they would make excellent eating.

Martin accepted the invitation with pleasure. "I'll spend Monday looking at used cars, and on Monday evening make a report." He looked at Cynthia for approval.

"That would be wonderful." Cynthia smiled back.

Martin drove Michael and the tools as far as the stable. All four horses who were grazing in the paddock galvanized as Emmy passed. Then, consumed with curiosity, they converged on the stable yard to watch while Martin helped Michael unload. Michael shook Martin's hand and thanked him, then turned to reassure his friends, who by now were gawking over the fence and trumpeting forth their suspicions of Emmy along with inquiries as to whether Michael had suffered any ill effects from such close contact with her. With a bang which sent all the horses flying, Emmy took off. She turned onto the State road and, popping merrily, bounded away toward Wolverton.

The weather on Sunday was unsettled. Fortunately the rain held off until the ceremonies at the Family Plot were completed. The civic authorities of Wolverton all put in an appearance along with a battery from the National Guard, which, after the speech and the placing of the wreath, fired ten deafening commemora-

111

tive salvos. Early in the proceedings, Martin Drew was spotted by Bugsy at the edge of the gathering, but during the salvos he disappeared and did not turn up for refreshments at the house afterwards.

"He probably hurried off to telephone his story to his newspaper," remarked Mrs. Armistead as the family washed up after the guests had left, "and it's just as well. There were barely enough cupcakes and cookies to go around. Those people ate as though they hadn't tasted good home-baked food in years."

"They probably hadn't," said Cynthia. "Not as good as yours at any rate."

The old lady smiled modestly into her dishwater. "I dare say you are right. Of course, I use only the best ingredients: our own eggs; milk, cream, and butter from Mr. Roote, and the other things from Anderson's Market.

Cynthia was drying teacups for Maggie to put away. Casually she asked, "Did Mr. Anderson let you charge again?"

"Yes, of course he did." Mrs. Armistead swished the teacups through the dishwater. "But" — she paused in her swishing — "he said he'd rather I didn't charge any more until we'd paid something on our bill. He was polite but firm. I don't like to worry you, my dear, but what are we going to do?"

"I've been expecting that," replied Cynthia. "Well" — she shrugged — "we'll have to use some of the money from the Pierce. I hope Martin can find some inexpensive sturdy car or truck that will do for hauling feed

112

and running errands. Living here so far from town, we can't get along without some kind of car. There's nothing more we can sell, except —"

"Not Stardust," cried Maggie in sudden terror.

"No, no," replied Cynthia. "I was going to say the furniture. We wouldn't sell Stardust even if we were starving, and anyway you need her to get to and from school."

"Safer and cheaper than any motorcar," muttered Mrs. Armistead into her dishwater.

Bugsy came in pushing the carpet sweeper. "There were hardly any crumbs because the dogs had got there first, but I went over the rugs anyway. Can I go now?"

"Yes, you may both go," said Cynthia, "and thank you for being such a help."

"I'm going to do my homework," announced Maggie virtuously. "It's too late to work out Star, and, anyway, it's raining."

It was not until she was in her room looking around for her schoolbooks that Maggie remembered. They were lying somewhere in the woods. It had rained Friday night. It was raining now, and night was falling. Maggie sank onto her bed and buried her face in her arms.

# 11

ON MONDAY morning, late (she had wasted an hour looking in the woods), and with a heavy heart, Maggie entered Henry William Armistead High School. Her first class was Algebra, and she got through it with nothing worse than the routine tardy slip which must be presented to Fried Egg before the end of the day. Mr. Patterson, an idealistic young man who believed that his students all loved equations as much as he did himself, simply asked for volunteers to demonstrate problems on the board. It never occurred to him to probe around for shirkers and duffers. The next class, French with Mlle. Cummington, was a different kettle of fish.

Mlle. Cummington combined Gallic impatience with a New England sense of duty, and she was an inspired prober. It took her only a few minutes to find the sore spot in her class. Once found, she applied herself rigorously to cleaning it and making it heal. Before she had finished with Maggie, on that fine spring morning, she had lectured on hard times and the price of textbooks; she had coached Maggie through an explanation (more or less in French) of how she had come to lose her valuable books. Now being pretty well wound up, she recommended in free-flowing French that Maggie crawl on hands and knees to Mlle. Eliot, bare all, and beg for mercy. Not — Mademoiselle had seemed about to finish, but had only been getting her second wind — that Maggie had any right to expect mercy, and so on, until, mercifully the bell rang.

In the corridor, Elizabeth, all friendship now that Maggie was in trouble, took Maggie's arm and offered to share her O Henry during recess. They sat in the sun on the side steps while Elizabeth commented briefly and unfavorably on Mademoiselle.

"At any rate, she forgot to give us homework, only being her, she'll remember and post it on the board."

"Oh well." Maggie chewed the O Henry and took comfort. "I'm not afraid of what Fried Egg will say any more because it couldn't be as bad as that."

"At least," said Elizabeth, "it won't be in French." She shook her head in a tolerant, elder-sisterly manner. "Honestly, Maggie, horses will be the ruin of you." As Elizabeth shook her head, a diadem of little curls waved and fluttered on the top of it, and Maggie remembered.

"Your hair looks nice," she said, "only queer. I mean different. I'm not used to it." Feeling that for all her good intentions she wasn't doing well, Maggie hurriedly asked, "How was the date?"

Elizabeth beamed. "Of course you must be dying to hear about it. I was waiting for you before school to tell you, but you were late, and then there was that awful French." She rolled her eyes and shrugged in what she believed to be the Gallic manner. Maggie couldn't help giggling. "You must be dying of curiosity," Elizabeth repeated, "and I won't keep you on tenterhooks any longer. Getting the permanent was terrible. She pulled my hair, and it was hot, and they only had one movie magazine, and it was three years old. When I got home my father said I looked like an Easter egg. I began to cry. Who wouldn't after what I'd been through? My mother got mad at my father, and she said he was mean and should try to give me confidence instead of taking it away (as if he could, but she meant well), and he said he didn't mean to be mean, but he liked me the way I was before, and my mother said he must realize that I wasn't a little girl any more (it's about time), and my father sort of fell into his chair and said, Yes, he must, and he'd raise my allowance a nickel a week if I'd just stop crying and believe that he was sorry he'd ever opened his mouth. All of a sudden it was almost time for Robert, and we hadn't eaten or anything. Not that I could eat by then. I got dressed in my good silk print and my spectator

116

pumps, and I brushed my hair very loose because it was sort of flat on my head. When I came down to show the family, Dad said I looked beautiful, which was very sweet of him, and actually I did look nice. Mother said I should eat a sandwich. I said I couldn't. She said I must. I said I couldn't. Dad said I was probably nervous. Mother said that was all the more reason that I should eat a sandwich. I said I couldn't. Dad said why didn't I just try? I said did he want me to throw up on my first date? He said no of course he didn't. All he wanted was a little quiet. Then the doorbell rang and I had to dash upstairs again so as not to seem to be ready."

"Why?" asked Maggie.

"Why? Honestly, Maggie, don't you know that you should never be ready when your date arrives? You should be called, and then you wait a minute and come downstairs. Well, never mind. You'll learn sometime." Elizabeth drew a deep breath and gazed off across the athletic field. "Have you ever noticed Robert Appleby's eyebrows?"

"No," replied Maggie, who had never noticed Robert Appleby, let alone his eyebrows.

"They turn up at the ends," murmured Elizabeth.

Maggie waited politely for her to go on. Elizabeth continued to gaze across the athletic field.

"So what?" asked Maggie.

"They're cute," replied Elizabeth, "but where was I?"

"You came down the stairs and there was what's-his-name with his eyebrows turning up at the ends."

"Yes," murmured Elizabeth, untouched by Maggie's sarcasm, "there he was, and the first part of the evening was perfectly awful. It was worse than anything I have ever been through."

"Come off it, Liz. Stop being like that."

"Like what?"

"Crazy. First you go into a tailspin about his eyebrows, and then you say it was awful. I haven't got all day. Tell it straight."

"I am," replied Elizabeth, "and I'm not crazy. You just don't understand. The first part was awful. Now listen and try to understand. We walked down to the Rialto, and Robert told about his trip to Washington with the Boy Scouts, which was all right except that when I tried to tell him about my trip to Nova Scotia, he acted as if I hadn't said anything and went right on about the upper and lower chambers, whatever they are!" Elizabeth shuddered. "We finally got to the Rialto, and the movie was divine — Clark Gable and Jean Harlow. I can't tell you how divine it was." Elizabeth screwed up her eyes, drew a deep breath, and let it out in rapturous puffs. "Robert bought popcorn and then he held my hand."

"So you couldn't get any popcorn?"

"No, of course not. Really, Maggie, you're terribly naïve." Elizabeth paused for a minute, lost in admiration of her vocabulary, then hurried on. "We got out of the movie and started to walk to Ray's for ice cream, and Robert started right off again where he'd left off about the upper and lower chambers. Well, we got to

Ray's, and there was a break while we ordered double chocolate malteds, but I could see he was going to start off again. I think he'd written it down beforehand and memorized it. Honestly I do. Well, at that point, I just took the bull by the horns. I leaned over the table at him, and I fluttered my eyelids and made my voice husky like Jean Harlow, and I said, 'Robert, let's not talk about Washington. Let's talk about us!' He jumped and looked embarrassed, and I said, 'Washington's O.K., but I'd rather talk about our own problems. After all, we're the coming generation, and our problems are important.' "

"What did he say?"

"He said his problems were important all right, but he thought I just tore around being beautiful and happy and didn't have any."

"That's right, isn't it?" sighed Maggie, suddenly reminded of her own heavy burden.

"It certainly isn't," cried Elizabeth. "I don't know how you can say that when you know what I go through with my family. My life is terrible, and so is Robert's. You see, we're both only children, and I tell you, Maggie Armistead, not being an only child yourself, you've no idea how perfectly hideous it is. We agreed it was the responsibility that got us down. After all" — she threw out her arms in a gesture of despair — "we're all the poor things have," and she fixed Maggie with a tense and tragic stare.

Maggie lowered her eyes. Feeling inadequate in the face of such deprivation, she muttered that it must be nice to know someone like Robert who knew what it was like too.

"How right you are," said Elizabeth. "If anything can preserve our sanity (I mean Robert's and mine), it will be our friendship," and she drooped there on the step with the utter weariness of one who has been struggling to preserve her sanity.

Maggie had rather hoped to consult with Elizabeth about her financial difficulties, but it was obvious that Elizabeth, in her present depleted condition, would not be much help. Instead Maggie managed to borrow *Graded Précis Work* and *Julius Caesar,* some paper and a pencil. She also managed to get the Latin and English assignments. This was not easy. Elizabeth's memory was cloudy about everything except what she had said to Robert and what Robert had said to her. On that subject her recall was total. When the bell rang again, they took their places in the study hall. Elizabeth opened her French book, rested her chin in her hand, and gazed mistily out the window, while Maggie applied herself to the strenuous task of preparing two subjects in one study period.

All during the noon recess Fried Egg was so busy that not until school let out at three-thirty was Maggie able to present her tardy slip and explain that she had lost her books. Fried Egg, limper and even more exasperated in her office than in the classroom, signed the tardy slip, found four new books in a cupboard, and without so much as raising an eyebrow, informed Maggie that she owed the Wolverton School System eight dollars and eighty-five cents.

"Bring me the money as soon as you can. Here's the bill." With a flap of her hand she presented a paper to Maggie and dismissed her.

Maggie found herself back in the corridor with the new books in her arms, the bill in her hand, and despair in her heart. Elizabeth was copying the French assignment from the bulletin board.

"I told you she would," remarked Elizabeth as Maggie approached. "Well" — she looked into Maggie's gloomy face — "what did she do to you?"

Maggie handed her the bill.

Elizabeth whistled. "That's tough, really tough. Will you have to use all the money you've saved for the horse show, or will your family pay it for you?"

Maggie leaned against the bulletin board. "I can't ask the family. I've got to raise the money myself."

Elizabeth sighed. "I know how it is."

Though it struck Maggie that Elizabeth hadn't the faintest idea how it was, she was grateful for any interest or sympathy. "You don't know of any jobs in town that I could do after school, do you, Liz? I'd do anything."

"If I knew of any jobs, I'd be out trying to get them myself, but there aren't any. Even Robert, who's sixteen, can't get a job. Robert says —"

Maggie didn't feel up to hearing what Robert said. "I was afraid of that. I guess I'd better start home."

Elizabeth ignored the interruption. "Robert says that

121

if he doesn't win the essay contest and get a little recognition and financial independence, he's going to run away."

"What essay contest?"

"Right there." Elizabeth nodded at the bulletin board. "It's the same old one. I don't blame him, and I feel the same way. How can they expect us to knuckle under, year in year out?"

Maggie stopped listening because she had found the announcement of the essay contest on the bulletin board.

"Mrs. Pinkingham, desirous of encouraging literary pursuits among the young people of Wolverton —" Maggie skimmed over a long paragraph about Mrs. Pinkingham's will until she was brought up short by the statement that the Wolverton Women's Club was offering four cash prizes of twenty-five dollars each. She read this over twice and rushed on with quickened interest to the rules of the contest. A prize would be awarded to the member of each class in Henry William Armistead High School who submitted the best essay in his class on a literary subject. The essays must not exceed forty-five hundred words, and they must be handed in by May 10, which, Maggie calculated, was two weeks away. A wild hope sprang up in her heart. Twenty-five dollars would do the trick, would take care of everything. For an ecstatic moment Maggie saw the judge walking up to her as she sat on Star's back. In one hand he held a blue ribbon, in the other a purse. Maggie shook herself and read through the rules again. All she needed to know was what a literary subject was, and how to write an essay. She turned to Elizabeth for help and was surprised to find her still talking.

"I said, 'But Robert, how can you possibly understand Pound well enough to write forty-five hundred words about him? I mean that's a lot. It really is. It may not seem a lot just to count, but when you start having to think up each word, then you notice it.' He was awfully cute, and he said that maybe he didn't understand Pound completely, but he understood more than any old dodo of a judge they could find around this town did, and he could say what he liked, and they wouldn't know the difference, which makes it easier. He said I was right to take Wolfe for my subject. He doesn't go for Wolfe himself, but he sympathizes with him. Of course, I think Wolfe is divine."

Elizabeth stopped to breathe, and gave Maggie the chance to ask, "Are pound and wolf literary subjects?"

"If they aren't, I'd like to know who is?"

Maggie was grateful to have learned that Pound and Wolfe were people. Concealing her ignorance with a show of nonchalance, she pursued her inquiry. "Who are Pound and Wolfe anyway?"

"Don't you know?"

"Should I?" Though she could feel her cheeks flushing with embarrassment, Maggie managed nevertheless to give a careless shrug.

"Yes," replied Elizabeth sternly, "you should. Everyone who isn't a complete boor should. Pound is *the* most important poet, and Wolfe is *the* most important novelist of modern times." She favored Maggie with a condescending nod. "Are you entering the contest?"

"Yes, I guess I will." Maggie felt surer of herself now that she had some idea of what a literary subject was.

"What's your subject?" asked Elizabeth.

"I haven't decided yet."

"You'd better hurry up. It's over in two weeks."

Maggie scowled. "They don't give you much time, do they?"

"They've given us six weeks. The notice has been up for a month."

"Oh, has it?"

"Honestly, Maggie, hadn't you seen it?"

Maggie shook her head.

"There, you see," Elizabeth pounced, "it's just what I said. You don't pay attention to anything any more except yourself and your horse."

"I've been schooling her for the show."

"No one minds that," scolded Elizabeth, "but when you don't notice anyone else, or hear what they say to you, or remember that they are alive even, then it does get pretty annoying."

"I'm sorry." Maggie bowed her head and asked, "You know about these things. Can you think of a subject that I could write about?"

"No. You'd better pick a book or a writer that you already know a lot about because you haven't much time."

"Will any book or author do?"

"Almost any, but it's got to be literary."

"I read a good book about stable management in the winter. Would that do?"

"No."

"I was afraid it wouldn't."

"You must have read some books," said Elizabeth more kindly.

"I guess I have, but I can't think of them."

"I'll tell you what I'll do to help you," declared Elizabeth. "When Robert telephones me tonight (he telephones me every night because my family absolutely refuses to let me out on week nights as if I was a babe in arms) — where was I? Oh, yes, when he telephones, I'll ask him if he has any ideas. He does have some awfully good ideas."

"Thanks, Liz, I'd be glad of any ideas," said Maggie, "though even if I get a good subject, I don't see how I have a chance to win with people like you and Robert in the contest too."

"Robert isn't in our class," Elizabeth corrected her gently, "so you don't have to worry about him, and of course I'm going to do my best, but I'm not infallible, and, well, there's no harm in trying." She smiled encouragingly.

"Thanks," said Maggie. "I — I guess you're right, Liz. I've been thinking too much about myself and Star. I guess I seem pretty selfish. Thanks for helping me, and" — Maggie swallowed her last vestige of pride — "thank Robert too."

Elizabeth seized Maggie's shoulder and gave it a friendly shake. "We'll do all we can for you. After all, you still are my best girl friend."

On this encouraging note they parted, and all the way to the stable Maggie searched the list of book titles in her memory (it was not a long list) for one which might serve her now.

# 12

Bugsy climbed down from the mounting block.

"I'm glad you've come. The reds must have driven out the blacks because there's not a one left, and it's been dull just sitting and waiting. Well, do you have to pay?"

"Eight eighty-five."

Bugsy whistled. "I don't see how you can get together that much."

"Neither do I," replied Maggie, "but I've got one chance. There's an essay contest. Come on. I'll tell you about it on the way home."

They were entering the woods by the time Maggie

had finished telling. Bugsy had listened carefully and now he shook his head.

"Of course, if you won, you'd be all set, but I don't see how you can. Even if I helped you, I don't think you'd have much chance."

Maggie nodded in gloomy agreement. The slight hope and confidence which Liz's interest had fostered began to fade. "I can't even think of a subject for an essay, and I don't know how to write an essay anyway."

"Don't give up. I didn't mean you should give up." Bugsy reached over in his saddle and patted Maggie's knee. "I just mean we can't count on twenty-five dollars. We've got to have reserves to fall back on." He sat for a moment with head bent. "I'm going ahead now to catch Miss Urquhart before she leaves to go home. I've got to tell her about not disturbing my butterflies in the study anyway, and at the same time I'll ask her for a loan."

"I don't think you should, Bugsy."

"I've got to," replied Bugsy. "I've been trying to borrow money all day. I asked some of the kids at school. Some of them ordered cocoons, but nobody had four dollars and seventeen cents to lend out all in a lump." He sighed. "I asked George Crosby, and he got mad. I tried to ask old Mr. Crosby, but I couldn't wake him up. Miss Urquhart's all that's left."

Maggie said nothing, but shook her head.

"I'm going to offer her interest," said Bugsy. "No one could ask for more than that."

He gathered up his reins and arranged his two nets,

one in his right hand, the other in reserve under his thigh. "If I see any good butterflies, I'll go after them. I'd give you the extra net, but I think you ought to think."

"Yes," agreed Maggie.

"Maybe you'll think better on horseback," suggested Bugsy.

He fetched Pansy a clout on the rear. With an ill-natured grunt she broke into a canter and carried him down the track and out of sight. Star tossed her head and pulled at the bit, impatient to follow, but Maggie held her back.

"I've got to think," she told herself. "I've got to."

Along the track, between the trees just bursting into leaf, Maggie walked Stardust, while with bent head and knit brows she tried to think. The sun first warmed, then burned the back of her neck. Stardust capered about and fretted at her bit. Maggie shortened her reins and ignored Star's protests. When, coming round a bend, Stardust spied Emmy parked by the side of the track, she made no attempt to control her feelings. Pretending to be even more terrified than she was, she jumped, landed stiff-legged, and as an afterthought jerked her head down so that Maggie could fly off more easily. When Maggie stayed aboard, Star turned herself into a sort of rocking horse and rolled and pitched, with jolts, side steps, and wiggles thrown in to make it more uncomfortable. Giving a cry of annoyance, Maggie got her horse in hand and, as a punishment, forced her to walk right up to Emmy and look her over. Stardust let on to find Emmy both terrifying and disgusting. She approached at a stiff, reluctant crawl with her neck stretched to a length more becoming in giraffes than horses. She rolled her eyes and flattened her ears. When Maggie, still administering discipline, forced her to touch Emmy with her nose, and Martin Drew popped up like a jack-in-the-box in the back seat, it was no more than Star had expected, but she went to pieces anyway. She reared, swiveled round on her hind legs, reared again, came down hard, and bolted. Maggie, fine horsewoman that she was, lost control. Martin, carrying a book and a blanket, clambered out just in time to see the horse and rider whiz around a bend and out of sight. He stood for a minute rubbing his eyes and blinking. Then he yawned, stretched, and crawled back inside Emmy. He had no sooner resettled himself with book and blanket than the clop-clop of horse's hoofs caught his ear. Peering out, he saw Star and Maggie returning. Maggie's lips were set in a firm line, and Star looked chastened. Maggie walked Star right up to Emmy and made her stand still with her nose against Emmy's chassis. Martin, bolt upright now, found himself staring full into the long, bony face of Stardust. When at last Maggie turned the horse away, Martin realized that he had been holding his breath. Although his reason assured him that horses were essentially gentle creatures who kicked only with their hind legs, he had felt that both he and Emmy were in imminent danger of being laid low with the blow of a hoof or the toss of that long, hard head. Maggie dismounted, tied Star's

130

reins on her neck, and told her to stand. In friendly fashion she approached Emmy and leaned in the window.

"She almost dumped me that time. It was my own fault for not paying attention, but I couldn't let her think she was getting away with it."

"I see," replied Martin.

"I've got to ride her out on the roads more before I enter her in the show. She's young and she's not very used to cars and she gets excited." Maggie grinned. Then as her eye fell on Martin's book, she became serious. "You write articles and things, don't you, Martin?"

"Yes."

"Do you ever write essays?"

"Yes, sometimes."

"What exactly are essays?"

Martin thought a minute. "They are short compositions which express the writer's personal feelings about something. The skill of the writing in an essay is more important than the actual subject matter, which may be quite trivial." He eyed Maggie curiously. "Does that answer your question?"

"Yes, thank you, I guess so." Maggie heaved a sigh. "I guess I should be glad the subject isn't very important because so far I haven't been able to think of one."

"Are you planning to write an essay?"

Maggie nodded. "It's for a contest. It's got to be on a literary subject."

"That shouldn't be too hard. You just write your

personal feelings about a book you've read or an author you are interested in."

"The trouble," confided Maggie, "is that I can't seem to remember having read any books for an awfully long time, and there isn't time to read books and write an essay and get Star ready for the horse show too."

"Then why not skip the essay?"

"Oh I wish I could," cried Maggie, "but, well, I'll explain it all, if you'll promise not to tell Gran and Aunt Cinny, and, of course, if I'm not disturbing you. I guess you were reading or sleeping. Gran thinks you should get lots of sleep."

"Don't worry about disturbing me now," said Martin. "Come in," and he opened Emmy's door and made a place for Maggie on the seat beside him. Martin listened carefully to Maggie's tale of high hopes laid low by financial reverses. When she had finished, he whistled and shook his head.

"You certainly could use that twenty-five dollars."

Maggie agreed.

"Have you ever read any poetry?"

Maggie shied and gave Martin a sideways, suspicious glance. Confronted with poetry, she behaved like Star confronted with Emmy.

"I'm just asking you because you haven't much time, and most poems are shorter than novels. You wouldn't have to spend so long reading."

"I haven't read many poems, and I didn't like the ones I read."

"Why didn't you like them?"

"I didn't know what they were about."

"If you found poems about something you did know about, do you think maybe —?"

Maggie scowled.

"Say, about horses?"

"Well, perhaps, but they'd have to be good."

Martin looked down at the book he was still holding. He smiled. "Did you ever hear of Wallace Armistead?"

"Wallace Armistead?" Maggie frowned. "Oh, you mean Great-uncle Wally. Of course I've heard of him."

"Have you ever read any of his poems?"

"No, but Gran and Aunt Cinny were talking about him just a few nights ago. I didn't listen much, but I think Aunt Cinny said she liked his poems. Gran felt sorry for her."

"Felt sorry for her?"

Maggie nodded. "Poor Aunt Cinny never gets to ride any more so she has to read poetry."

Martin studied Maggie's frank, worried face. "Is that what your grandmother said?"

"She didn't say it, but it's what she meant. If I could buy back Amber, or just any fairly good horse for Aunt Cinny, I'd be so happy!" Maggie sighed. "You see, that's partly why I wanted so much to put Star in the Junior Hunter Stake. I know she'd win the fifty dollars, if I could just get together the entry fee. I thought I could do it somehow, but now, with the books to pay for too, I've just got to enter this essay contest and try to win, even if I haven't a chance."

"I think you have a good chance," replied Martin.

133

"What I think is that you should write an essay on the poems about horses by Wallace Armistead."

Maggie balked. "Gran says he couldn't tell one end of a horse from the other."

"I have great respect for your grandmother, but in this particular case, I think she may be wrong."

Maggie still hung back.

"There are only three poems about horses, and only one of them is at all long." Martin tapped the book he was holding and smiled encouragement.

"Do you really think they are good poems about horses, I mean ones that tell the truth?"

"I think they are very good," replied Martin, "but I'd like to know what you think because on horses you are something of an expert." He held the book out to Maggie. "If you'd like to read over the horse poems now, you may use my book. I was reading it before you came."

Maggie was not immune to flattery. She accepted the book.

Martin opened Emmy's door. "I want to pump up the tires," he explained, "because I'm going to leave her here all evening and walk the rest of the way to your house for dinner." He took off his coat and rolled up his sleeves. "She has some slow leaks."

"Of course," Maggie smiled, "you are coming for dinner, and we're having chicken. We can go the rest of the way together. I'm hungry already."

"How about reading the poems first?"

"Oh yes." Maggie's smile faded. "You're sure they

aren't very long? She eyed the book in her hand. "What are they called?"

"They are called 'Red Pepper,' 'The Well-Behaved Pony,' and 'Horsey of Woodfield.' You've plenty of time to read them through now while I fix Emmy." He reached the tire pump out from the floor and slammed the door shut. Maggie sat imprisoned with the poems of Wallace Armistead and no choice but to read.

Martin pumped all Emmy's tires, not forgetting the spare. He unscrewed her radiator cap, squinted inside, and screwed it carefully on again. He couldn't afford to lose any more radiator caps. They were getting scarce, and he'd been to several used-car lots before he'd been able to buy this one. As a final attention to Emmy he opened her door, pushed up the front seat, and, taking the ruler he kept for the purpose, measured the gas in the tank. Emmy was all in order. Martin replaced the ruler, wiped his hands, and put on his coat.

"Well" — he studied Maggie, who was sitting bolt upright in the back seat with her eyes glued to the book — "how do you like them?"

Maggie was startled. "Like them?" she repeated. Slowly a smile spread over her face. "Oh, I do like them. You know, they're the only good poems I've ever read."

Martin grinned. "I thought you might like them."

"Gran was the only one who could really manage Red Pepper, even though he belonged to Grandfather," exclaimed Maggie, "and she had to watch him every minute. She's told me about him."

"You think that Red Pepper in the poem is a horse that your grandfather and grandmother really owned?"

"Of course, and the pony sounds like Sweet William. He had beautiful manners when he wanted to."

"And is Horsey of Woodfield another one of the horses?"

"No, not a horse. It's Gran."

Martin opened his eyes very wide. "Good grief," he murmured, "and I never thought of it."

"There are parts though" — Maggie shook her head — "that I don't understand at all. I don't understand some of the words, and I don't see why, when it starts off so well with Gran taking a horse over the hunter training course, it has to get all mixed up."

"So that's what's happening?"

"Yes, I'll show you where the course was. It ended in the old cellar hole, and I guess that's the part the poem is talking about when it gets mixed up and says that Horsey galloped through the house, knocking over the furniture and scaring the people. I think it's silly." Maggie tossed her braids. "It was just the old stone foundations that Gran fixed up for banks and walls to train her hunters. The house hadn't been there for years, and there weren't any furniture or people. Uncle Wally just dreamed that part up."

Martin began to laugh. "Do you know that you've just explained a line in that poem that has bothered me and a lot of other people for years?"

"I'm glad I could help you." Maggie eyed the book with satisfaction. "I guess I'm better at poetry than I thought I was. I love the parts about Gran riding. They make me feel almost as good as if I were riding too." She smiled. "But" — and the smile faded — "it's not going to be easy writing forty-five hundred words."

"Don't worry," replied Martin. "You read the poems over some more and think about them. We'll have another talk about them later. Right now" — he looked at his watch — "we should be starting along, and I wish you would show me that cellar hole on the way."

Maggie's eyes lighted. She handed the book back to Martin and jumped out of Emmy.

"You know what I'll do? I'll jump Star down the bank and over the walls at the cellar hole for you. It'll be just like the poem. Star is still young, and she's never taken those jumps before, but you'll see, she'll jump just as well as those horses of Gran's."

# 13

By THE TIME Maggie and Stardust had polished off the bank and the wall to their mutual satisfaction, the monuments and the shaggy old lilac in the nearby Family Plot were casting their shadows across the road. Martin, Maggie, and Stardust set off again toward the house. Maggie chattered excitedly about Star and the ribbons she was going to win, while Martin nodded, smiled, emitted sympathetic grunts, and pursued his own thoughts. Stardust was the first to hear the silvery cascades of laughter which tinkled intermittently from the woods and kept pace with them. She pricked her ears and, remembering Emmy, whinnied suspiciously.

Out of the woods skipped what looked to be a girl of twelve. Her hair was a cloud of gold. She wore an old-fashioned white pinafore over a dark frock and carried a bunch of pink arbutus. Running up to Star she laid a friendly hand on the bridle, and Star, reassured, made a pass at the arbutus. With a silvery giggle, the child snatched the flowers away and turned her smiling face to Martin. Martin caught his breath, for the face he was looking into was not that of a child, but of an elderly woman.

"Hello, Miss Urquhart," said Maggie. "I bet you've been following us all the time. What are you doing out here anyway?"

"I'm a sly boots," giggled the little creature. "Madam sent me to pick arbutus for the table. Such lovely birds, and we are eating in the dining room, and charlotte russe. Whipped cream! Macaroons! Like the old days!" Miss Urquhart screwed up her eyes and smacked her lips. She opened her eyes and let them rest on Martin. They were as blue, as sunny, and as placid as two ponds in a sheltered valley.

"Is that him?" Miss Urquhart whispered to Maggie.

"Excuse me." Maggie remembered her manners. "Miss Urquhart, this is Mr. Drew."

"Pleased to meet you," said Miss Urquhart with a bob of her head, which jolted the golden cloud of hair down onto her forehead. Quite unabashed, she pushed the cloud back where it belonged and beamed at Martin, displaying pink gums and a scattering of teeth.

"The pleasure is mine," replied Martin with a courteous bow. He studied the ruddy face, creased and wizened, but sound, like a good winter apple in February. The blue ponds returned his glance. No ripple or shadow marred their beautiful serenity.

"Haven't we met before? I seem to remember —" Martin paused.

"Ah!" Miss Urquhart's eyes radiated pure joy. "The gentlemen don't forget me. 'With her hair like flax and her eyes like the sky,' that's what Father used to sing about me, and I held the horse, and he beat the shoe, and the sparks flew up!" Miss Urquhart jumped high in the air and waved her arbutus. Her laughter rang like a peal of fairy bells.

Martin could not conceal a start.

"Her father was the blacksmith," explained Maggie.

"I must be wrong," murmured Martin. "For a minute I seemed to remember —"

"Remember," repeated Miss Urquhart. A cloud passed over the sunny surfaces of the ponds. "There's something to remember." She looked here and there and up and down until her eyes fell again on Star. The cloud vanished. Standing on tiptoe by Maggie's stirrup, she gestured to Maggie to bend down so she could whisper to her.

"No, Miss Urquhart," said Maggie firmly, "I can't let you do that."

Miss Urquhart jumped up and down while she whispered harder.

"But maybe they won't," said Maggie, "and maybe

140

I won't, and I can't let you give us money, Miss Ur- quhart. I can't."

Miss Urquhart clung to the stirrup. "His plan," she cried aloud. "Hope of the family. Brain!"

"Yes," replied Maggie wearily, "but Bugsy doesn't know everything. Thank you, Miss Urquhart. I'm very grateful, but I've got a plan too."

"Everyone has a plan," said Miss Urquhart. "I had two plans when I came out." Again she searched about. "I had two plans, maybe more," she assured Maggie.

"Of course you did," said Maggie soothingly, "you planned to get arbutus and to tell me Bugsy's plan."

"That must be it," replied Miss Urquhart, relieved. Her eyes shone yet more radiantly. "I saw the horse jump over the wall!" She crouched, bounded forward, then, giggling happily, looked up to Maggie for ap- proval.

"She jumps as well as Red Pepper, or Fancy, or Am- ber, or any of them, doesn't she?" demanded Maggie.

"She jumps better," cried Miss Urquhart with a wave of the arbutus, "better than any of Madam's —" she stopped short. "It was Madam had the plan." She sucked in her breath. The pools grew dim and trou- bled. "Where is it?" she asked. "Ah," she pointed the arbutus at Martin, "it's him." Once more the pools re- flected pure sunshine. "Madam had a plan that I get back in time to open the door for him. Don't move!" Playfully she shook the arbutus in Martin's face. "Give me to twenty." She steadied her coiffure, waved the arbutus, and was off.

141

"I guess I should explain to you that she is sort of cracked," said Maggie as the little figure flitted round a bend and out of sight. "They say a horse kicked her in the head when she was young. We're used to her, but I guess maybe she frightens people who don't know her."

"She did startle me at first," admitted Martin, "but I'm used to being startled. As soon as I got over my first fright, I began to find her charming." He smiled at Maggie. "Just as, after my first fright, I found you and your horse charming."

"We're not as crazy as she is," replied Maggie quite seriously, "and she's not as crazy as you might think. She knows a lot about horses. I guess she picked it up hanging around the blacksmith shop. You heard what she said about Star and how she jumps better than Gran's horses did? Well, I bet it's true." Maggie was off again. She talked about Star until they drew up under the porte-cochere. Here Martin turned up the steps.

"Please tell them I'll be right along," said Maggie, "but don't tell them anything else. I'll tell about the essay contest when I get in. That will please Aunt Cinny, but I don't want her to know the rest." Maggie sighed gloomily. "I'd forgotten what a mess I'm in."

Martin promised not to tell and tried to persuade her that the mess might not be so bad as she thought. Maggie trotted away toward the stable.

Martin pulled the bell handle. At the feel of the smooth brass knob, remembrance of his very first visit

142

to Woodfield flooded his mind. He had been diffident then, and a little awed by that knob and that massive door. Stronger, however, than any doubt or fear had been his hope that as he entered that door he would enter into the mystery which surrounded the name of Wallace Armistead. As the gong throbbed deep inside the house, Martin's heart throbbed again as it had, so long ago, with a wild and wonderful excitement. The door swung open, and there stood Miss Urquhart, panting. Borne along on the tide of his memory, Martin stepped inside.

"I made it," confided Miss Urquhart.

Martin's face lighted with a smile. "It was you who opened the door the first time I came here."

Miss Urquhart smiled coyly back. "The gentlemen always remember me."

Still immersed in memories, Martin nodded and smiled dreamily until those memories carried him on inexorably to the denouement of that first, long-ago visit, and his smile became rueful. He shook himself.

"I just come part time," Miss Urquhart was confiding in him, "to accommodate." She threw a quick glance behind her and went on in a whisper. "You know they lost it all, poor things. I'd do anything for them. They're all I've got. I am an only child." Her eyes beamed their sunshine on Martin.

"Did you know Mr. Wallace Armistead too?" asked Martin at a venture.

The sunshine of Miss Urquhart's eyes shone more serene, more wonderfully bright. "Mr. Wallace," she whispered, "my only love. Always true." Smiling like an angel, Miss Urquhart fell into a trance.

Cynthia Armistead came from the dining room with a bottle of sherry and glasses.

"Hello," she said. "I hoped it was you. I wasn't sure because I didn't hear Emmy." She cast a shrewd glance at Miss Urquhart, who was still in her trance. "Miss Urquhart," she called gently, "Miss Urquhart, Madam needs you to help with the gravy. Run along like a good girl."

Miss Urquhart came to with a giggle and skipped away to the kitchen.

In the drawing room, close to the log fire, it was warm and cheerful. Cynthia poured sherry.

"This is very special because there isn't much left." She handed a glass to Martin. "Father laid down a large cellar in 1918 so he'd be one up on prohibition. It should have made him happy, but it didn't." She shook her head. "I can still remember how he roared and whacked the table when he tasted his glass of wine and remembered that he couldn't order more. He drank only one glass a day, at dinner, and I figured out that at his rate he had enough to last him seventy-two years, six months, and four days."

"Did you tell him, or were you too scared?"

"I was scared, but I told him. He was delighted. He laughed out loud. The next day he gave me Bluebell. He was very kind in his way."

"Shall we drink to his memory?"

"Yes." Cynthia raised her glass. "But wait," she said,

"until my mother comes. It will make her so happy to hear you propose a health to Father's memory."

"Then to another great Armistead" — Martin raised his glass and looked hopefully to Cynthia — "Wallace Armistead."

"Yes," replied Cynthia with enthusiasm, "to Wallace Armistead."

While the fire crackled and they sipped their sherry, Martin made Cynthia laugh again and again as he described his encounters with Star, Maggie, and Miss Urquhart, and went on to tell about his day at the used-car lots. The more he talked, advising her, answering her questions, the more comfortable and happy he felt. When Mrs. Armistead entered from the kitchen, hot, tired, and worried about the sauce, Martin touched and delighted the old lady by proposing a health to the memory of Henry William Armistead. Her spirits revived, and so did her confidence in the sauce. When Bugsy appeared, sullen at having been forced against his better judgment to wash his neck and change his shirt, Martin was happily inspired to describe the two most promising used cars he had seen. They were a 1929 Ford pick-up in good shape for one hundred dollars, and a 1930 Chevrolet coupé with a rumble seat for one hundred and fifty.

Bugsy immediately saw the possibilities of these vehicles as butterfly-hunting conveniences. His eye lighted. He saw himself standing, net poised, in the rumble or the pick-up, while the Ford or Chevy bowled along a country road. His sharp glance darted here and there, missing nothing. "Stop!" The driver slammed on the brake. Bugsy jumped to the ground. In a matter of minutes he had netted his butterfly. Back into the rumble (or pick-up), a shout to the driver, and they were off again. How much more comfortable and efficient than Pansy! Bugsy's sullenness vanished. He delighted his aunt and grandmother by the gracious way in which he thanked Martin for helping them to find a new car. Martin felt happier than ever.

Maggie announced her return by shouting, "Here I am," and clattering upstairs, presumably to change the Colonel Roosevelt breeches for something more formal. It was some time before she came down. She had not changed her attire, but she was carrying her aunt's copy of Wallace Armistead's poems.

"It took me a long time to find the book," she explained. Then she proudly announced the essay contest and the subject of her proposed essay.

"Maggie," exclaimed her aunt, "I'm so happy that someone else in the family is interested in Uncle Wallace's poems. Don't worry about winning the contest. Just think about understanding and enjoying the poems and writing about them as well as they deserve, and, if you do that, you are sure to win."

Mrs. Armistead took a different view.

"If you stick to the horses, you'll be all right. There was so much Wally didn't know about horses, it would fill a book, let alone an essay." She became fidgety. "Do you think she's forgotten about announcing dinner? The sauce will spoil if she doesn't hurry. Poor old thing," she explained to Martin, "I only keep her because she's like one of the family and she needs the money. Her father was the last good blacksmith in the county. I have to look after her. Ah, here she comes."

"Dinner is served," announced Miss Urquhart in an excited, silvery quaver.

"Thank you, Miss Urquhart," Mrs. Armistead boomed back. Rising, she took Martin's arm and led the way to the dining room.

# 14

DINNER WAS a huge success. The chickens were moist
and tender. The asparagus, first of the season, melted in
the mouth, and the sauce which had so worried Mrs.
Armistead came smooth, golden, and perfect to the
table. Martin praised each dish as he tasted it, while
Maggie and Bugsy made indistinct sounds of appreci-
ation.

"Be careful," Cynthia warned them. "This is the
dining room."

"I can't help it," replied Bugsy. "It's so good."

The spaniels, overflowing with hope and saliva,
sneaked in from the kitchen and clustered about the

knees of Mrs. Armistead, who tried to conceal them under the tablecloth. When she thought Cynthia wasn't noticing, she fed them bits of boned chicken from her plate. Miss Urquhart divided herself between serving in the dining room and devouring a private feast in the kitchen. She flitted so nimbly back and forth that her golden cloud could barely keep pace. At each reappearance, her ruddy old face glowed more radiantly with accumulated happiness and butter. When Maggie, her first hunger allayed, described Star's reaction to Emmy, Miss Urquhart, bubbling over with joy, acted out the part of Star. Stiff-legged and crafty-eyed, she angled up to the sideboard, tossed back her head in sudden terror, reared, and galloped into the pantry. Her giggles could be distinctly heard tinkling on and on just behind the pantry door.

Cynthia laid down her fork. "I think I had better go out and try to quiet her."

She half rose, but too late. Bugsy, not to be outdone by his sister, had already risen. With swoops and swings, he was describing how he had chased and lost the first Compton Tortoise of the season. Miss Urquhart, with her arms outstretched like wings, was back in an instant, a butterfly now. She darted, fluttered, swooped, and soared round and round the table. It was some time before Mrs. Armistead and Cynthia could coax her back to the kitchen. While Maggie cleared the table, they managed to quiet Miss Urquhart until she was steady enough to bring in the charlotte russe.

"I was sure she'd drop it," said Mrs. Armistead when

everyone was served and Miss Urquhart had retired, "but it would have broken her heart not to be allowed to carry it in."

"If she had dropped it," replied Martin, "I should have cried."

"She'd have cried too," said Bugsy. "She loves whipped cream, and she told me this afternoon that she doesn't get it very often."

"I think she can manage the coffee," continued Mrs. Armistead, "but you children must be very quiet. Don't stir her up. I hope she'll be able to wash the dishes without breaking them." She turned to Martin. "You seem to have excited her."

"I didn't mean to. When she opened the door for me tonight, I remembered that she opened it when I came here ten years ago. I told her I remembered. She seemed pleased."

"You didn't say anything about Wallace Armistead, did you?" asked Cynthia.

"Yes, as a matter of fact, I did." Martin paused and frowned thoughtfully. "She was more than pleased at that. I guess you'd say she was carried away."

Cynthia laughed softly. "That was it. Uncle Wally must have been especially kind to her in the old days. She still remembers him and worships him. Just the mention of him, and she's carried away."

"We were all especially kind to her," said Mrs. Armistead. "I don't know why Wally impressed her more than anyone else."

"She says he understood her," explained Bugsy. "He

told her their minds worked the same or something like that."

"That sounds just like Wally. As if her head wasn't addled enough to begin with." Mrs. Armistead gave a snort of exasperation, then turned to Bugsy. "Since you and Miss Urquhart are so chummy, will you please go to the kitchen and tell her quietly that we are ready to have coffee?" She rose, gave her arm to Martin, and led the party across the foyer to the drawing room. A subdued Miss Urquhart passed the coffee cups without mishap. Bugsy and Maggie sat very genteelly on the edges of chairs to either side of the coffee tray. Without making the slightest disturbance or attracting anyone's attention, they managed to steal three sugar lumps each out of the bowl and suck them noiselessly down to nothing.

Mrs. Armistead poured herself a second cup of coffee. "Now, Martin, what is this business that you want to discuss?"

Maggie stood up. "May I be excused? I've got homework."

"Yes," said Cynthia, "and, Bugsy, you must go to bed in half an hour."

"Yes, Aunt Cynthia," replied Bugsy dutifully, "I'm going right up," and he began to work his way back into his chair where in comfort and obscurity he could listen to the discussion of business, a subject in which he was interested.

"I'll try to be short and to the point," began Martin. "At present there is a great deal of interest in Wallace

Armistead's poetry. Articles and books about him, no matter how poor, are snatched up by publishers and gobbled down by Armistead fans."

"Blinco and P.H.," exclaimed Mrs. Armistead, nodding wisely at Cynthia.

"Exactly," replied Martin. "Ten years ago Mr. Henry Armistead had letters written to him by his brother. He was going to show them to me, but I said the wrong thing, and" — Martin shrugged — "you know what happened."

"What did you say?" asked Cynthia. "I've always wondered."

"I said," replied Martin with a little smile, " 'Sir, you must feel very humble when you remember that he was your brother.' "

"Great heavens," exclaimed Mrs. Armistead, "you were lucky not to be killed outright!"

"Yes," replied Martin, "I was young and inexperienced, and I worshiped Wallace Armistead."

"I know you did," Cynthia interrupted. "You told me about it when we took that long walk, and you made me want to read the poems. I did, as soon as I got home. I'd never looked at them before."

"And you liked them, didn't you?"

Cynthia nodded. "I've been reading them ever since." She leaned toward Martin. "Don't you remember? While you and Father were talking about Uncle Wallace I said that if Father would just read the poems, he'd understand why you admired them so."

Slowly Martin smiled at her. "Yes, now I remember. He sent you to your room. I should have taken that as a warning, but I didn't. It just made me feel happy and bold because you liked the poems too." His smile faded and he frowned at the carpet. "I'm sorry for everything. Without meaning to, I seem to have set off a tragic train of events."

"Don't feel sorry," Mrs. Armistead intervened. "You couldn't help it any more than Wally could himself. It goes back so far and is so mixed up that we might as well call it chance or bad luck and be done with it. Now just what is this business?"

"Oh, yes." Martin gave his head a businesslike jerk. "I am commissioned by a well-known and highly respectable publishing company to buy those letters for any price within reason that you want to name."

"There are no letters," replied Mrs. Armistead.

Martin looked long and hard at the old lady, and she returned his look. Martin dropped his eyes. His hands worked on the arms of his chair. "If you do not choose to sell the letters, that is your affair, and — and," he stammered, "my business is finished."

"It's not a matter of choosing," said Mrs. Armistead. "There just aren't any letters."

Martin bowed his head.

Quickly Cynthia reached out her hand and touched Martin's. "I know it's hard to believe." Her voice was pleading. "I know you think it isn't possible that letters which we all saw in my father's hand shortly before he died should have vanished after his death. I know you think we are hiding something, but, believe me, we aren't. There are no letters."

"How do you explain?"

Cynthia shook her head. "I can't explain. On the morning after Father's death, his study was locked and sealed. It remained locked and sealed until after the funerals. Mr. Purinton and I broke the seal and went in together to find the will and read it. Together we went through all Father's papers. Everything was in order. I looked for those letters particularly, because I knew that you thought they were valuable. After I had searched every corner of the room, I looked in the shrubbery outside. There was nothing there. I looked in the fireplace. Father never had a fire. The grate was empty. There was no trace of anything having been burned."

"Did you look in the wastebaskets?" piped Bugsy from the depths of his chair.

"That was the first place I looked, and, Bugsy, you should be in bed."

"Did you ask Miss Urquhart?"

"No, why should I?"

"She was working here then. Martin remembers her. She probably went through all the wastebaskets before she went home for the night. She always does."

All three grownups stared at Bugsy. "I never thought of that," murmured Cynthia.

"That's funny," replied Bugsy, "I did. Right away.

And," he went on, "if she did take the letters, she still has them. She never throws any of her papers away. She says that when you are educating yourself, you never know what may —"

"Where is she?" Martin jumped up.

Cynthia jumped up too. "I think she is still in the kitchen."

"Now wait a minute," boomed Mrs. Armistead. "If you rush in on her now asking about letters and Wally, there's no telling what she'll do, except you can be pretty sure she'll break all the dishes. You won't find out anything, though."

"That's right." Cynthia sat down again. "We must approach her very gently and carefully."

"Where does she live?" asked Martin. "I'll drive her home and ask her casually on the way."

"She lives in the blacksmith's house, and she always walks home by a short cut through the woods," replied Mrs. Armistead. "Nothing would disturb her more than for you to drive her home. She's not used to motorcars. Now sit down, Martin, and calm yourself."

Martin sat down.

Bugsy stirred in his chair. "I could probably ask her so she wouldn't get excited. She likes me."

Again the three grownups stared at him.

"You are probably the only one who could," said his grandmother. "Go ahead."

A half hour later, Bugsy returned from the kitchen. With head lowered in assumed modesty, he crossed to the fireplace before turning to face his audience.

"Well" — Mrs. Armistead thumped her cane — "what did she say?"

Slowly Bugsy raised his head. "She has some letters."

"Are they written by Wallace Armistead?" Cynthia asked.

Bugsy nodded.

"Will she sell them?" Martin leaned forward in his chair.

Bugsy raised a restraining hand. "She doesn't want to part with them."

"Why not?"

Bugsy fluttered the restraining hand. "She doesn't care about money. The letters mean a lot to her. They're all she has —"

"Stuff and nonsense!" cried Mrs. Armistead. "The poor thing's not responsible. Bugsy, you go out to the kitchen and tell her that I said —"

"Gran" — Bugsy fixed the old lady with a round, accusing eye — "you asked me to handle this."

Mrs. Armistead snorted, threw back her head, thumped her cane, but subsided.

"And did you try to persuade her?" asked Cynthia diffidently.

"I was coming to that." Bugsy cleared his throat. For a minute he savored the satisfaction of holding his audience in suspense. "She said," he went on, "that if I brought Martin to her house sometime and watched him all the time to be sure he didn't run away with them, she might let him see her letters."

Martin drew in his breath and leaned forward.

"I'm as anxious as any of you to get Miss Urquhart to sell her letters," Bugsy went on. "In fact, I've a special reason of my own." He stopped and licked his lips. "But I won't talk about that now."

"How soon do you think she'll let me see the letters?" asked Martin.

Bugsy pursed his lips. "Of course, I can't guarantee that she'll actually show them to you." Martin nodded and sighed. "But" — Bugsy modestly lowered his eyes — "I've arranged for us to go to see her tomorrow afternoon."

"Good! Good for you!" Martin's face lighted, and getting up, he shook Bugsy's hand.

Bugsy's chest swelled, and a pink glow suffused his countenance. "She has confidence in me," he murmured.

"So do I," replied Martin.

Bugsy's pink glow grew pinker. "We can start tomorrow, as soon as I get home from school."

"I'll be waiting for you."

Cynthia laughed. "I'm excited too," she admitted, "and I congratulate you, Bugsy, and I wish you both luck, but" — she raised her eyebrows and nodded significantly at Bugsy — "it's late, and tomorrow there's school."

With a sigh, Bugsy kissed his aunt and grandmother good night. He shook Martin's hand.

"Tomorrow," he said, "at about four-thirty."

# 15

WHEN BUGSY and Pansy reached Woodfield at four-thirty the next afternoon, a Model A pick-up truck was sharing the shelter of the porte-cochère with Emmy. Martin came out the front door and down the steps.

"Your grandmother thinks it's less unsettling for Miss Urquhart if we take the short cut through the woods, and if you ride your pony. Shall we start right along?"

Bugsy cast an interested eye over the Model A. "Is that it?"

Martin nodded. "We bought it this morning. When we get back, you can look it over. If we hurry along, there may even be time to take you for a ride later."

Bugsy tried to turn Pansy back toward the woods, but Pansy was looking forward to food, rest, and the conversation of her peers. She put down her head, got the bit firmly between her teeth, and kept straight on toward the stable. Forgetting that he was afraid of horses, Martin grabbed her bridle and, before she realized what was happening to her, had turned her and was dragging her off in the opposite direction. Pansy was a strong-minded pony. She flattened her ears, threw up her head, and braked with all four feet. Martin tugged in vain, then, being pretty strong-minded himself, he looked about for a whip. Bugsy had left his net in Crosby's stable, and there was nothing suitable in sight. Martin let go of Pansy, reached inside Emmy, and emerged brandishing her gasoline ruler. At sight of the ruler, Pansy lifted her head higher, the better to laugh. Martin beat away at her flank. Pansy sat tight and flicked her tail in scorn. Suddenly the ruler snapped in two, the halves flew high in the air, and one of them came down squarely on Pansy's uplifted nose. Pansy jumped two feet into the air, then bolted. She was halfway to Miss Urquhart's before Bugsy could stop her and wait for Martin to catch up. For the rest of the way Pansy went as fast as she could, apparently taking strength and comfort from the sound of Martin's hard and painful breathing as he sprinted behind. They approached Miss Urquhart's residence from the back. After jumping over a broken stone wall, cantering across an abandoned pasture and around a tumble-down ell which had once been the smithy, Pansy and Bugsy drew up at the hitching post by the front door. Bugsy tied Pansy and waited for Martin to catch up.

The blacksmith's house as well as his smithy had fallen into disrepair, and it fronted on a curve of road which had been cut off in order to straighten the State road. Now, after years of disuse, the abandoned curve was overgrown with weeds and pitted with holes. Breathless though he was as he rounded the ell, Martin could not but notice the forlorn and desolate appearance of the place. Bugsy led the way up a weedy front walk and banged on the weather-beaten door.

After a few minutes the door opened enough for Miss Urquhart to stick her head out.

"I'm glad it's you." She opened the door a little farther so her visitors could squeeze in. "I knew someone was coming, but I wasn't sure who it was." She glanced up and down the stretch of abandoned road before shutting and bolting the door.

She was dressed somewhat gaudily in a gown of soiled green satin embellished with swirls of orange beadwork. On her feet were pink satin opera pumps. Both pumps and gown were too large for her. Teetering in her pumps, she confronted her guests. Her smile twitched uncertainly. She patted her coiffure, plucked at her beadwork, and fumbled at the neck of her gown, which hung loose and slippery on her tiny shoulders.

"Did you have a plan?" She turned the lovely blue pools on Bugsy. Their serenity was somewhat misted over. "Count on me, whatever it is," she added vaguely, then, taking comfort from the presence of Bugsy, she nudged Martin. "Hope of the family." She winked. "Brain." She tapped her forehead.

"We do have a plan," Bugsy encouraged her. "Don't you remember, Miss Urquhart? We talked about it last night at Woodfield."

The mist dissolved, and Miss Urquhart's blue pools shone out in all their lovely serenity. "I remember so much at Woodfield. Father used to say, 'Sunny' (that's what he called me, though it's not my real name) 'is like an elephant even though she is so tiny. She remembers everything,' and the sparks flew up and the big horse from Woodfield tossed back his head." Miss Urquhart tossed back her own head and jumped right out of the pumps. When she had readjusted her coiffure and got back into the pumps, she remembered her duties as a hostess.

"Please to come into the parlor," she said primly, "and make yourselves at home. I'll remember anything you like."

The hall had been chilly after the sunshine outside, but in Miss Urquhart's parlor was stored the cold and damp of eternal winter. With a gracious gesture Miss Urquhart indicated the parlor suite, done in black horsehair and deployed with military precision about the parlor stove. "Please be seated," she said. "This is the best parlor. We have two. The Urquharts have always held their heads high." She gave a genteel little sniff.

Martin and Bugsy sat down carefully, trying to choose

161

places where the horsehair was not ripped.

"It is very nice here," said Martin politely. "Has this always been your home?"

"Always," replied Miss Urquhart. "This is my home." The mist gathered again over her eyes. She turned to Bugsy. Her silvery voice quavered, almost broke. "How can they take me to a home when I have a home?"

Bugsy had unfortunately sat on a broken strand of horsehair. It was sticking into him and he writhed miserably on the sofa until with a jerk he disengaged himself.

"They can't." His voice rang out in relief.

"You won't let them," declared Miss Urquhart.

Questingly Bugsy eased himself along the slippery horsehair until he found a new and safer location. He braced his feet so he wouldn't slide down onto the floor.

"No," he declared firmly.

"Hope of the family," murmured Miss Urquhart. "Brain." She tapped her head, shook it admiringly at Bugsy, and seemed to shake her anxiety away. "They can't take me away." The mist lifted from the pools. "I'll run into the woods and hide until they go off. I know a place they'll never find me." She giggled and plumped down on the horsehair beside Bugsy. "What does he want?" She jerked her head toward Martin.

Dust rose from the horsehair. Bugsy sneezed and almost slid off his seat.

"Don't you remember, Miss Urquhart? Try to remember."

"Anything you like. Count on me. I remember how Father used to say —"

"No, not that." Bugsy braced again with his feet. Mustering his patience, he spoke gently, but firmly. "What you must remember is that last night you promised me that if I brought Mr. Drew here this afternoon, you'd show him your letters from Mr. Wallace Armistead."

Miss Urquhart laid her hand on a beadwork swirl in the vicinity of her heart.

"Ah, Mr. Wallace."

Terrified that she'd go into a trance before he'd finished his business, Bugsy plucked at her skirt. "You know you promised."

Miss Urquhart gave him a crafty, sideways look. "Did I cross my heart and hope to die?"

"Yes, you did."

"I won't let him take them away in a car." Miss Urquhart set her jaw. "I won't let them take me away in a car. They wanted to take me away in a car," she laughed slyly, "but I gave them the slip."

"He won't take the letters away in a car, and we won't let anyone take you away either," Bugsy tried his best to reassure her.

"I don't want to force you," put in Martin. "I just want to look at your valuable letters. I admire Wallace Armistead almost as much as you do. Just to see his handwriting will mean so much to me."

"You promise you won't grab them and run away?"

163

"I promise," said **Martin**. "Cross my heart and hope to die."

"I think I can trust him." Miss Urquhart nudged Bugsy, then leaped to her feet.

Bugsy sneezed again. "You can. Please get them." He started to get up.

"Stay where you are," Miss Urquhart commanded. She crossed to a door at the back of the room. On the threshold she turned. "This is my study. I have papers. They're private." She clopped out, closing the door behind her.

Martin and Bugsy had plenty of time to observe Miss Urquhart's best parlor in all its shabbiness. Bugsy's eyes roamed gloomily from a broken pane of glass stuffed with rags to a hole in the ceiling plaster, and back to the cold, rusty stove. He shivered, braced with his feet, and sneezed.

"I didn't know she was this poor. She's even poorer than we are. She couldn't loan us money even if she remembered that she said she would, and I think she's forgotten."

Martin tapped his feet to keep warm. "From what she said, I'm afraid the town authorities are planning to move her to the poorhouse or the asylum. I expect they think she can't look after herself."

"She couldn't stand that," Bugsy sighed. "We can't let them."

"You've got to persuade her to sell those letters," said Martin. "With the money from them, she can get the house repaired, buy coal, and live very comfortably. No one can take her away then." He smiled encouragingly at Bugsy.

Ten minutes later, Bugsy, who had been sneezing at ever shorter intervals and was shaking with cold, could stand it no longer. He tiptoed to the door by which Miss Urquhart had left them, and, sliding it open a crack, peeped through. When he turned back to Martin his eyes were bulging with astonishment.

"There's a room full of papers piled right up to the ceiling," he whispered. "There's just a passageway through the stacks of papers to another room with more papers. She's in there somewhere. I can hear her tapping and rustling things." He sneezed.

"Sh," warned Martin.

Miss Urquhart appeared in the door. "I said, 'No peekies!'" She shook a handful of papers at Bugsy. The pools were ruffled with doubt.

"I'm sorry." Bugsy hung his head. "I was looking for my handkerchief," and without seeming to try, he sneezed again.

Martin caught his breath lest now, at the last minute, she would take offense. She teetered uncertainly in the doorway. Bugsy gave her a long appealing glance and wiped his nose on his sleeve.

"Brain," she murmured at last. "Hope of the family." From somewhere inside the green satin gown she extracted a grayish handkerchief which she handed to Bugsy. Her pools beamed once more with sunshine. She tripped over to Martin holding out the papers. His hand trembled as he took them. He recognized the

165

handwriting at a glance. It was Wallace Armistead's. His eye sped over the first page.

"Dear Miss Urquhart: Next time you wash my shirts, please, no starch. W. A."

Hastily Martin turned to the next paper.

"Dear, dear Miss Urquhart: Again NO starch in my shirts, please! It makes me itch. W. A."

Martin scanned the third and last paper.

"Dear, dear, dear Miss Urquhart: Once more, I don't want starch in my shirts. What I tell you three times is true. Your irritated but ever hopeful W. A."

Martin stared at the papers, sighed, shook his head, and sighed again. With a shrug and a dim smile, he handed them back to their owner.

"Thank you very much. They are very interesting."

"They are mine." Miss Urquhart pressed them to her heart.

"You are very lucky to have them," replied Martin.

"Dear, dear, dear Miss Urquhart," she smiled. "He understood me."

"I don't suppose," asked Martin sadly, "that you have any other letters written by Wallace Armistead?"

"He went away, but he left me these." Miss Urquhart's voice rang soft as a distant silver bell. "They are all I have, but they are enough for me to remember him." Her eyes cast their radiance into another world. She gave a sigh of pure bliss. "Dear, dear, dear Miss Urquhart!" She was entranced.

"Don't you want to buy them?" demanded Bugsy.

Martin shook his head. "These aren't the letters I was commissioned to buy."

They took leave of Miss Urquhart, who accompanied them to the door and waved goodbye without emerging from her trance. Martin and Pansy with Bugsy on her back trudged in silence toward home.

"Maggie will just have to win that contest," declared Bugsy at length.

"Um," muttered Martin absently. He walked with head bent, wrapped in his thoughts. Suddenly he began to laugh. "Dear, dear, dear Miss Urquhart," he chuckled. "The old fox is determined to remain a mystery. He's probably laughing right now, wherever he is."

"He's dead," Bugsy reminded him.

Martin nodded. "You're right, as usual, and it's time I forgot all my silly fancies and went back to work."

"Don't go back to work."

"It's work or starve for me," replied Martin good-naturedly, "and my vacation with pay ends on Friday."

"You can stay here," said Bugsy. "I've been thinking that you might be interested in investing —"

"No!" Martin stopped short and shook his finger at Bugsy. "I'd like to stay here. In all the world, I'd like nothing better, but I've got to work for a living. Invest!" He laughed. "I've invested my vacation with pay. It was all I had. In my way I'm as poor as Miss Urquhart, and probably just as crazy."

With a combination of shrewdness and tact which did

credit to his distinguished ancestry, Bugsy made no further attempt to touch Martin for a loan. He did not, however, give up. He slumped on Pansy's back staring thoughtfully at her ears.

"I was a fool to get so excited," Martin murmured to himself. "She was excited, too." He sighed. "It serves me right." He walked on slowly.

Bugsy continued to stare at Pansy's ears. His eyes bulged with concentration. Slowly he straightened in the saddle. He smiled faintly.

"I don't think you are a fool," he ventured. "I think you're on the right track. There are still all those papers in Miss Urquhart's back rooms. You haven't looked through them yet."

Martin stopped short. "You mean that the right letters, the ones I want, might be in with the papers you saw piled to the ceiling?"

Bugsy nodded. "They're what she's collected to educate herself. It would take a long time to go through them, but —"

"If she'd picked those letters out of the wastebasket ten years ago, would they be piled up somewhere in her back room now?" Martin's eye lighted.

"Oh yes, she never throws anything away."

"But would she let me look through them?"

Bugsy thought hard, but could find no way out. "No," he admitted.

"Then I can't. Don't tempt me." Martin waved his hand and strode ahead.

"You could do it when she wasn't home."

"That would be housebreaking," retorted Martin over his shoulder.

"But you'd be helping her really." Bugsy kicked Pansy and followed close behind. "She needs that money. You don't want her to go to the poorhouse, do you?"

Martin didn't answer.

"The letters will really be lost then," added Bugsy. "I bet they'll take all the papers and burn them in the dump."

Martin shuddered, but walked on in silence. They were almost back at the porte-cochere when he turned and confronted Bugsy.

"I think you're right. I think the letters are some-where in that pile of papers, but I can't sneak into her house and steal them, even if it is for her own good." Martin shook his head. "I wish you'd never had that bright idea."

Bugsy's eyes almost popped out of his head while he wrestled with his conscience.

"Hallo! Any luck?" Mrs. Armistead's unmistakable voice reached them from the porte-cochere.

Bugsy relaxed. "There are Gran and Aunt Cinny waiting for us. Ask them. If they think it's O.K., then it is."

Cynthia and Mrs. Armistead listened with mixed amusement and sadness to the story of Miss Urquhart and her letters. Finally, with trepidation, Martin sub-mitted Bugsy's latest idea for approval. Cynthia thought a long time before she said:

"If you really think those letters are in with her rubbish, and if you know you can sell them for a good price, I think you should look for them, even though it's very like housebreaking." She turned to her mother. "What else can we do for her? We can't help her more than we do now, and we can't let her go to the poorhouse."

"Certainly not!" Mrs. Armistead thumped her cane. "I promised Angus Urquhart to look after his daughter, and I'll do it." She fixed Martin with a flashing eye. "If you can dig out Wally's letters and put them to a good use, go ahead, and I'll forgive Wally the trouble he's made."

"You already have forgiven him," Cynthia reminded her.

"Wally," declared the old lady, "needs a great deal of forgiving."

Accordingly, the Armisteads, with the exception of Maggie, who hadn't a moment to spare, devoted the next week to luring Miss Urquhart out, while Martin, who had decided to forget his own rocky finances, sneaked in and went about his stealthy work. At the week's end, Martin wasn't halfway through the pile. Miss Urquhart had been collecting for close on to thirty years, and her notions of filing were foggy at best. Martin realized early in the game that he must look at every paper in that vast collection before he could be sure of not having missed the only one he wanted. Having already invested so much in the search, he was determined to carry it on to the end.

Miss Urquhart worked out two days a week, one at

Woodfield, the other for Mrs. Roote. For the rest of the time, Cynthia persuaded her to take the air in the pick-up truck, Mrs. Armistead detained her with reminiscences of horses and blacksmithing in the old days, and Bugsy, as soon as he got home from school, lured her into the woods after butterflies. Martin scrabbled conscientiously through the papers. When he wasn't scrabbling, he repaired Mrs. Armistead's chicken coop and helped her plant a vegetable garden. He also found time to give Cynthia driving lessons. His strength was returning rapidly. He was busy, hopeful, and happy.

# 16

WHAT WITH the essay, the training of Star, the painting of the fences, and the daily grind of homework, Maggie was certainly busy, but not always hopeful and happy.

Elizabeth, when she first heard about Maggie's essay, showed more interest in Martin Drew than in Wallace Armistead. "You mean, Maggie, that you have this boy friend and haven't even told me?"

"He's not a boy friend." Maggie's eyes widened in horror. "Why, he's over thirty."

"Oh." Elizabeth's interest in him vanished. "I never heard of this Wallace Armistead, but I'll ask Robert if he has. Robert is awfully well read."

Robert had heard of him.

"Robert," reported Elizabeth with gloomy relish, "says that Armistead is the only modern poet that's more obscure than Pound. He thinks you're crazy even to attempt him."

"Martin doesn't."

"You just said he was over thirty. How can he possibly know anything about it?"

Maggie's eagerness and enthusiasm faded. A lump of anxiety swelled up in her stomach. When at recess she retired to the girls' coatroom to read over her three horse poems, they no longer held meaning or enjoyment for her. The words had become a nonsensical, jingling accompaniment to the words of Robert. "She's crazy to attempt it." The lump in her stomach waxed and grew heavier. At noon, because she couldn't eat, she went to the Henry W. Armistead Library and startled the librarian, who had never seen her at close range or off a horse, by checking out all the books about Wallace Armistead.

During the next week the lump was with her almost constantly. When she was schooling Star, perfecting her in backing, turning on the forehand, guiding her with the lightest of hand and the gentlest of pressure in and out between obstacles, over unfamiliar trails, along the hazardous, automobile-infested State road, or through the traffic of Wolverton Center, the lump was with her. When Star, who loved to jump, was flying over the bank and the walls at the old cellar hole, the lump got worse than ever, for the more Star jumped, the more surely

Maggie knew that they could win the Junior Hunter Stake and the fifty dollars, if only they could raise the entry fee. Every minute spent with Star was a minute lost on the essay, and the essay, hateful though it was, was her last hope.

Maggie only forgot her lump completely when, throwing responsibility to the winds, she helped Bugsy chase butterflies on their way home from school. Now ducking low in the saddle to squeeze under branches, now standing high in the stirrups to swing their nets, they swarmed through brush and swamp, across brooks, over walls, up hill and down dale. When the going got too thick for the horses, the children jumped off, and, with nets waving, chased the butterfly on foot. Then back into the saddle, shouting in triumph or disappointment, and on with the chase until both hunters and horses were exhausted. The season was still early, and the butterflies they caught were, for the most part, little Azures or drab Dusky Wings. They never did get a Compton Tortoise, though they pursued several.

Their only commercially valuable catches were two more battered Mourning Cloaks, no good as specimens, but valuable (so Bugsy hoped) for the eggs they would lay. He put them away in the study along with his other hopefuls and looked in on them frequently, though he couldn't expect caterpillars for another two weeks. As soon as the chase ended, Maggie's lump came back worse than ever. She had wasted valuable time, and, more disgraceful still, she had taken chances of hurting Star by driving her so wildly over such rough ground.

Unlike Pansy, who hated all forms of exercise, Star delighted in the chase. She pricked her ears hopefully at all flying objects, and as the net waved about her head, and Maggie yelled in excitement, Star jumped higher and ran faster.

One afternoon, while the children were saddling up to go home, George Crosby the younger came into the stable from his parking lot.

"See your aunt's got herself an old pick-up," remarked George to Maggie.

It was a warm, sunny afternoon, and Maggie was anxious to be off after butterflies.

"That's right," she replied and went on tightening Star's girth.

"Motor don't sound too good to me."

Maggie ignored this and fetched Star's bridle.

"Where'd she get it?" continued George.

Maggie fastened the throat lash. "I don't know. Some used-car place, I guess."

"Why's that young fellow that works for the government riding round with her all the time? Is he sweet on her or what?"

There was something so nasty about George's tone that Maggie flushed with anger.

"No, he isn't sweet on her, and he doesn't work for the government either."

"So they were lying to me," snapped George. "I thought there was something fishy about him."

Maggie mounted. Boldly from the elevation of Star's back, she replied, "He made the government story up.

We laughed like anything afterwards." She pressed her legs against Star's sides. "Come on, Bugsy."

George's angry reply was drowned in the clatter of hoofs. Maggie turned back to laugh and wave goodbye. As George watched the children trot away, his eyes narrowed, and a very unpleasant smile spread over his fat face.

By May fifth Maggie had read everything in the library about Wallace Armistead and had studied her three horse poems until she knew them by heart. It was time to begin to write, and the lump lay like a stone in her stomach. She hadn't the faintest idea what to say.

Almost in tears, she turned to Martin. "I've read. I've memorized. I've thought and thought, but I've nothing to say. I don't even know how to begin."

Having finished his daily stint with Miss Urquhart's papers, Martin was setting out tomato plants for Mrs. Armistead. After Miss Urquhart's dank rooms, he found gardening in the fresh air particularly agreeable. He received Maggie's communication with casual good humor.

"That's how every writer feels when he starts to write something."

"No they don't, or they never would. It's just me that can't write anything."

With a snort of anguish Maggie hauled a grubby handkerchief from a pocket of the T.R. breeches (she had just got home) and buried her face in it.

Martin was touched. He dropped his trowel, stood

176

up, and laid a kindly hand on Maggie's shoulder.

"Don't give up. Let's sit down and plan what you want to say and in what order." He led Maggie to a grassy spot at the edge of the garden and invited her to sit. "If you have a sort of outline in your mind when you start, it will help."

Obediently Maggie sat down. She put away the handkerchief and looked expectantly at Martin, who settled himself beside her.

"Now" — Martin pulled a blade of grass and began to chew it — "let's start at the beginning. You tell me now why, on that day in Emmy, when you first read the three horse poems, you felt that you could write an essay about them."

Maggie scowled at him. "I'm trying to remember."

"Take your time. Try to remember exactly what you thought to yourself when you read those poems for the first time."

"It was something like this. I'd heard about Wallace Armistead because he was my great-uncle. I knew he couldn't ride, and I knew he wrote poetry. I didn't much like poetry anyway, and I didn't expect to like his, but I read the three poems because you told me to." Martin nodded encouragingly, and Maggie went on. "I couldn't understand everything in them, but I could understand the parts about the horses, and I was surprised because he knew what he was talking about even though he couldn't ride. They were good poems. I kept reading them over, and they kept getting better."

"That's right," Martin nodded, "be honest. Now you must quote the lines that you knew right away were good and explain how you knew it."

"I don't know how I knew it."

"If you take the lines apart and study them word by word, it will help you to know."

"That's not the sort of thing Liz would do."

"What would Liz do?"

Maggie thought a minute. "She would tell how the great thoughts in the poems filled her with great feelings and brought home to her great truths."

Martin raised his eyebrows. "Do the great thoughts fill you with great feelings and so on?"

"No," admitted Maggie, "I can't find any great thoughts, but Liz says that's because —"

"Let's forget Liz," broke in Martin. "Let's stick to the poems. I think that after you have shown why the lines you liked right away are good, you should go on and explain how you have come to understand and appreciate the lines that puzzled you at first."

Maggie was silent for a time. "I have come to understand them," she said slowly, "but it's not because of great truths."

"Can't you forget great truths?"

"I'll try, but it's not because of social implications or moral fervor either, whatever they are." Maggie gave an impatient toss of her head.

"Forget them too."

"They are in the books about the poems."

"Forget them."

Maggie sighed. "It sounds sort of silly, but if you think about that horse Red Pepper and then about Grandfather, you can't help seeing that they're awfully like each other."

"Yes," cried Martin, "go on!"

"And the pony, Sweet William, who was so well behaved that Gran let him eat sugar out of the sugar bowl and talked to him as if he were a person, he was like Uncle Wally when he was staying here. No pony is really well behaved, and neither was Uncle Wally. He pretended to be, and underneath he was mean and tricky. He wasn't as big and important as the real horses, and he felt bad. Pansy's the same way. Gran was chief horse here. She was Horsey. She was the way a horse should be." Maggie rubbed her forehead. "I know it all sounds silly to you. It did to Liz."

"Silly!" exclaimed Martin. "It's the most sensible thing I've ever heard." He eyed Maggie with respect. "Nothing like it has been done with those poems since they were written."

"I wish it sounded more like the sort of thing Liz or those people who write books write."

"Be glad it doesn't!" Martin began to laugh. "It's a beautiful joke on everyone, including the clever fellows like me who thought they understood Armistead."

"There's something else. It's not a joke." Maggie bit her lip. "What will Gran say?"

Martin stopped laughing. "I see what you mean."

"What I'll be doing when I explain those poems," exclaimed Maggie, "is calling Gran and Grandfather names right out in public. She won't stand for it."

Deep in thought, Martin spat out his old blade of grass and pulled a new one.

"Well?" demanded Maggie.

Martin spat out the new blade of grass. His lips moved. He was reciting "Horsey of Woodfield" to himself. He shook his head, pulled a new blade, and chewed as if his life depended on it.

"Well?" Maggie asked again.

When Martin just chewed harder than ever, Maggie collapsed backwards into the grass. "I'll give up," she wailed. "I can't write it."

"You can't give up. You've made a discovery. Or rather" — Martin chewed more slowly "— "part of a discovery."

Flat on her back, Maggie emitted a groan worthy, in its anguish, of Liz herself.

Martin brought his fist down hard on the ground. "You've got to start to work." He spat out his grass. "With all the understanding you have now, you must read those poems over and over and concentrate on each word" — Martin pounded with his fist — "until you see what I think I see in those poems."

Maggie reared up from the grass. "Listen!"

Martin shook his fist at her. "It's there. I know it's there. You've got to find it for yourself. You've got to start to work."

"Work!" exploded Maggie. "What do you think I've been — ?"

"Work!" shouted Martin. "When you see what I see"

— he waved his fist at Maggie, then carried away by what he saw he waved it at the general landscape — "you can tell the world that Wallace Armistead made fun of your grandmother, but at the same time, and with a subtlety and humor of which only he was capable, paid her as great a compliment as a poet ever paid a woman."

# I7

"WHAT IS THIS?" The voice that had once rallied the
hunters and subdued the pack halted Martin's effusion.
From the edge of the garden plot, Mrs. Armistead and
Michael, holding a basket of chicken droppings between
them, fixed Martin with astonished and not very
friendly stares.

"We have not been eavesdropping," said Mrs. Armistead. "In fact, it's been impossible not to hear you."

Maggie still crouched in the grass, but Martin, carried
away by his enthusiasm, jumped up and ran to Mrs.
Armistead.

"Maggie is about to make a great discovery about
Wallace Armistead. When you read her essay, you will
really and truly forgive him."

"I have forgiven him. I've forgiven him a great many times. I'm getting tired of forgiving him. Right now, all I want to know is what you and Maggie are shouting about. First I hear Maggie say that Wally had called me and my husband names in public. Next you cry out at the top of your lungs that he paid me a compliment. If I'm to be in this essay of Maggie's, I think I want to know what's being said about me." Mrs. Armistead tapped with her cane, and her eyes roamed suspiciously from one culprit to the other.

"You must read the essay," replied Martin, happily oblivious to the old lady's annoyance. "That will make it all clear. Ah, Mrs. Armistead, how fortunate you have been! And to think that I have read and reread those poems and never guessed! The minute I set eyes on you I should have known."

"Martin," replied the old lady, "you make no sense at all. Maggie, see if you can explain this to me and make some sense."

Maggie shrank deeper into the grass. "I'm not sure I can explain. I haven't got that far along."

"Then explain as far as you have got. Stand up, speak out, and try to make sense."

Maggie stood up, but found it difficult to speak out and make sense.

Mrs. Armistead tapped with her good foot as well as with the cane. "Come, child, don't be afraid. It's not your fault if Wally called me names."

"I know it isn't, Gran, and I know you won't like what he said about you and Grandfather, but, really, when you think about it, the way Martin has, it isn't as insulting as it sounds at first. At least, I guess it isn't because that's the part I haven't —"

"For goodness' sake, Maggie, stop beating about. You are as bad as Martin. I don't want to know the part you haven't got to. I just want to know those names Wally called Henry and me."

Maggie drew a deep breath. "Well, he called you Horsey," and, as best she could, Maggie blurted out her interpretation of the horse poems of Wallace Armistead.

Mrs. Armistead punctuated this recitation with snorts, head tossings, and pawings of her cane.

"So," she exclaimed at the end, "Henry was right to lose his temper about that Horsey poem. I wasn't sure myself." She dropped her side of the basket and scowled at the ground.

Michael emitted something between a gargle and a chuckle and let go his side as well.

"Many's the time," he announced to no one in particular, "I said to myself in the old days, 'That Red Pepper and the Master are like as two sticks of dynamite, and just about as comfortable to have around. You never know what will set them off, and when they go'" Michael rolled his eyes and made an eloquent sound deep in his sinuses. "I always said that Mr. Wallace was cleverer than he let on." Michael clicked his tongue slyly. "He had a mean streak too, only it was quieter and ran deeper than the Master's. As for Madam —" Michael paused to clear his throat.

"So that's what those poems say?" Mrs. Armistead demanded of Maggie.

Maggie shuffled, writhed, and hung her head. Michael, however, hadn't finished.

"I was saying," he went on, "that even in the old days Madam wasn't like other ladies. She was taller, and stronger, and handsomer. She held her head like a Thoroughbred, and she wasn't afraid of man or beast. She could school the meanest horse, and she'd blow up the Master himself if he made a mistake handling her horses. She saw every bruise, every speck of dust, every dirty bit of harness." Michael lifted his old head, and his old eyes glittered. His eyes hardened. He turned on Maggie. "Not like the younger generation that leaves its horse standing when she's hot from exercise, and doesn't even remember to tie her so that she is wandering about, tripping on her reins." His eyes moved significantly from Maggie to Star who, with reins dragging, had just wandered around the side of the house.

"It's this awful essay. I forgot to tie her reins together. Otherwise she wouldn't have moved. I'll get her." Maggie started toward Star.

"No," commanded Mrs. Armistead, "I want to talk to you." She turned to Michael. "Please take Miss Maggie's horse to the stable for her. I'll spread the manure myself."

With a last accusing glare at Maggie, Michael departed. Mrs. Armistead frowned first at Martin, then at Maggie.

"Now that it's perfectly clear to everyone, even Michael, what names Wally called us, I'd like to know just how he managed to pay me a compliment. Go on." She jerked her head at Maggie.

Once more Maggie writhed, swallowed, and hung her head.

"Stand straight and speak out."

"The poems don't really call you names."

"I thought you said they did."

"That's just part of what they do. They say a lot of other things too. I mean they don't really say them, but they make you think of them."

"It seems to me that if Wally had wanted to say something, he could have spoken out. I've always spoken out. Henry always spoke out. When it came to calling names, Wally spoke out."

"But, Gran, Uncle Wally wasn't calling names. He was trying to say something that was too mixed up to just speak out. He was a poet."

Mrs. Armistead pressed her hand to her forehead. "You are not making anything clear, but, from what I can understand, I think that in your essay you had best just go on letting people think those poems about horses are really about horses."

"I told you so!" Maggie turned almost fiercely on Martin. "I might just as well give up. I'll give up the contest, and the horse show, and everything." Her voice rose. Abruptly she bit her lip and turned away.

"You don't have to give up," cried her grandmother. "Just stick to the horses and leave out the people."

Martin laid a hand on Maggie's shoulder. "Mrs. Armistead, let me try once more to explain."

Mrs. Armistead made an impatient gesture toward the garden and the basket of chicken droppings.

"I'll try to be clear and quick." Martin looked her straight in the eye. "I'll speak out."

"Yes," she replied, "speak out."

"Wallace Armistead and his brother were alike in that both had great energy and great ability, but their interests, desires, and aims, with one exception, were as different as night and day. The one exception, Mrs. Armistead, was you. They were both in love with you."

Mrs. Armistead caught her breath and half opened her mouth.

"You told me to speak out," Martin reminded her.

After a moment she whispered, "Go on."

"I think you can imagine how Wallace felt when his brother, so to speak, got you first. He knew quite well that you were much happier with his brother than you would ever have been with him, and yet, although years went by, he couldn't help loving you himself because, Mrs. Armistead, it was a habit. He had been in love with you, you see, ever since you were little children and played together around those cabbage roses at the back door." Martin paused and looked at her. "Isn't that so?"

Mrs. Armistead shook her head in a bewildered manner. "He made fun of me. He laughed at me."

"He laughed at you and his brother, but mostly at himself and his own unhappiness. What else could he do? In the end, when he couldn't laugh any longer, he managed to tear himself away. It was the only decent thing he could do."

Mrs. Armistead had been staring through Martin. "I never thought," she murmured. "I never guessed. He made me feel so — so uncomfortable, as if he thought I was funny, and yet, sometimes when he talked about the time when we were children, he was different." For a long time she said nothing. "If I had known, I'd have felt differently about those jokes he made. But how could I know? And what good would it have done me to know? What would Henry have done?" The old lady's eyes widened. "Perhaps Henry knew all the time." She stopped abruptly and shook her head. "I never understood Wally, and I guess I never understood Henry as well as I thought I did." She became aware of Martin again. "If you hadn't made me remember how Wally looked and spoke when he talked to me about the old days and the cabbage roses, I wouldn't have believed you. How did you know?"

"I've read his poems."

"I never could understand them," said the old lady. "Poor Wally." She leaned heavily on her cane and bent her head. After a silence, she looked up at Martin.

"Do you think that tomorrow you could drive me to the Family Plot and leave me there for a while? I would like to see how the cabbage rose I planted for Wally is getting along. I'll save out some chicken droppings for it. I wouldn't want Wally to think I'd forgotten him, or" — she paused — "that, now that I know, I'm not grateful and sorry."

Martin said he would be glad to drive her.

Mrs. Armistead continued for some minutes longer lost in her own thoughts. Finally she shook herself, drew a deep breath, and nodded briskly at Maggie.

"It's a good thing after all that you are writing this essay. When it is published in the *Wolverton Ledger,* everyone will know that Wallace Armistead wasn't just talking nonsense in those poems. They'll know that he loved in vain, and, on the whole behaved like a gentleman. They will know that Henry, except for some understandable fits of temper, behaved very properly too, and they will know that I am proud to have been loved by two such distinguished men." She straightened her shoulders, lifted her chin, and smiled. For a minute, the soft pink light of the setting sun suffused her aquiline face and spare figure with the softness and beauty of youth. "When do they award the prizes?" she asked.

"The essays have to be handed in in three days," replied Maggie. "I don't know when they'll give the prizes."

"I hope they'll make up their minds quickly. I hate dawdling. I want this thing to come out in public. It's only fair to Wally."

"Gran, I may not win, and then nothing will come out."

"Of course you will. Remember what I told you about the Armisteads all having hidden abilities? Writing essays is your hidden ability, just as cooking is mine." She glanced at the sunset. "Martin, if you can get in the rest of those plants while I finish spreading the manure, I'll be delighted to have you stay to supper. I've a nice meat pie ready to go into the oven."

"I'd like to stay very much. I'll get right to work." Martin smiled at Maggie. "There's no quitting now. You've got to do it."

Maggie rubbed her forehead. "I think I know what you mean about the poems, but I'm afraid."

"Don't be afraid, and don't write what you think I want you to write, or your grandmother wants you to write. You are the one who made the great discovery. You made it by yourself. Now you must understand it by yourself. When you do, you'll write a prize essay." He gave her an encouraging nod.

For a few minutes Maggie watched her grandmother tossing manure about with an energy that belied her years.

"I guess I've got to write a prize essay." She gave a businesslike hike to the T.R. breeches and with shoulders squared and braids jiggling marched toward the house.

At ten-thirty that night, Maggie huddled in bed wrestling with the opening sentence of her essay. A tap on the door startled her.

"Come in." She steeled herself for a scolding from her aunt.

But it was Bugsy. His clothing was disheveled and his eyes gleamed like electric bulbs in his white face.

"I saw your light, and I came to tell you. They're hatched."

"What?"

"They're hatched, and they're voracious."

"Who are?"

"The caterpillars. They're voracious. I went in after supper just to look, and all the leaves were covered with little ones. They were eating as hard as they could. I've been bringing more leaves to them ever since. It was hard because it was dark, and I couldn't turn on the light, and I had to go in and out by the window and get my water from the chicken house so no one would hear me."

Slowly Maggie took all this in. "Are there lots of them?"

Bugsy nodded, and, spreading out both hands, he wiggled his fingers expressively.

"They're voracious."

"How often do you have to feed them?"

"I don't know yet. They've got to have a steady supply of fresh leaves. Willows, poplars, and elms are what they like best." He looked at Maggie's books and papers. "I guess you're pretty busy. I don't suppose you'll have time to help me collect for them."

"I can't until I've finished this."

"When's it got to be finished?"

"Friday. After that I'll help."

"Thanks. It's awfully important that they get enough at this stage."

"How long is this stage?"

"About a month."

"The horse show will be over before they even start to make their chrysalises."

Bugsy sighed. "I hoped I could borrow on them, but so far I haven't been able to. I'm not much help to you now, but, Maggie, when all those chrysalises hatch into perfect specimens, each one worth from three to five cents —" Bugsy drew a deep breath, and a smile lighted his wan face. "You'll see. It will be worth the trouble."

"Of course it will. Now go to bed and let me work."

"I'll get Miss Urquhart to help me collect food," said Bugsy, lingering at the door.

"Good. Now go to bed."

"How's the essay coming along?"

"I don't know yet, but I've got some ideas."

"Do you think you can win?"

Maggie rolled her eyes. "If I don't, I'm done for. Now, for heaven's sake, go to bed."

# 18

At 3:00 a.m. on Friday, May 10, Maggie finished copying her essay. At 9:00 a.m., she dropped it in the contest box.

Elizabeth, as soon as her own essay had slipped through the slot, was seized with dizziness, palpitations, and stomach cramp. She squirmed in her chair as she waited with Maggie for French class to begin.

"Oh Lord, I know I should have done that middle part differently. What I said stinks. It positively stinks. I felt it so deeply, but it stinks. I think I'm going to be sick." She clutched at her abdomen, and her head lolled back. "It's so terribly final," she gasped.

"I'm glad it's final," declared Maggie.

"Aren't you going bughouse? Aren't you nauseated? What's the matter with you anyway?"

"I'm too tired," replied Maggie, "to feel anything," and she had the misfortune to yawn just as Mlle. Cummington entered the room. Mademoiselle took this as an affront to *la belle France,* to *la belle langue française,* and to herself. Maggie spent the next forty minutes in a linguistic agony of atonement.

A good night's sleep restored Maggie to her usual spirits. The horse show was three weeks away, and Star's training had been neglected. She put the contest out of her mind and devoted her full attention to Star. Her aunt, who appeared more carefree than she had for years, shared Maggie's concern for Star's education. Regularly, in the late afternoon, she met Maggie and Star at the old tennis court to watch and criticize their performance. Martin turned up as regularly as Cynthia. He stood beside her watching and listening, and although he protested that he hadn't the faintest idea what they were all doing, he seemed to enjoy himself. At some time during each session, Cynthia found it necessary to mount Star in order to demonstrate a point of form or to get the feel of a problem that bothered Maggie. Maggie admired her aunt's riding.

"She's out of practice," Maggie explained to Martin, "but she's terribly good. See how light her hands are. There's no one else I'd let ride Star so soon before the show."

Martin nodded. "You are very fond of her, aren't you?"

"Oh yes."

"I don't suppose you could get along without her."

"No," cried Maggie. She turned to Martin with a worried frown. "I'd rather be dead."

"I meant your Aunt Cynthia, not Star."

"Oh." Maggie paused. "But it doesn't make any difference. I couldn't get along without her either." She gave a little shiver. "Please don't talk about that sort of thing. It frightens me."

"I'm sorry." Martin bent his head, and, having apparently lost interest in horsemanship, he continued to stare at the ground while Cynthia finished her demonstration.

During this time Martin got the habit of dining with the family almost every evening. Mrs. Armistead prepared wholesome dishes to build him up. To show his gratitude, he brought presents of candy and other delicacies which gave a festive quality to the dinners. These were eaten cozily, in the kitchen. While the big stove glowed and popped, and the spaniels, ever hopeful, slobbered about Mrs. Armistead's knees, everyone talked, laughed, and ate with gusto. The conversation skipped from horses to motorcars to Michael to horses to butterflies to Miss Urquhart to poetry to horses to gardening to the old days to the present to the future, and always back again to horses. Somehow only the happy, hopeful, or humorous aspects of these, or any subjects, seemed important. Occasionally, after dinner, Martin and Cynthia drove off in Emmy to see a movie. This pleased Mrs. Armistead.

"I like to see her getting out," she confided to the children as they helped her to wash up. "Martin's as safe a driver as I've seen, and his car is steady. It does your aunt good to see these moving pictures and forget her responsibilites."

One evening, she confided further that in the late summer when, as a result of Cynthia's good management, they had a little spare cash, she was going to buy a pig from Mr. Roote. He had promised her the pick of the litter and at a very reasonable price. She had always wanted a pig and had planted turnips with one in mind. It would be a nice surprise for Cynthia on her birthday.

Maggie and Bugsy exchanged nudges and winks because their birthday surprise for their aunt was so much nicer, and, for the moment at least, seemed certain of accomplishment.

Each night, after checking his caterpillars, Bugsy lay down to dream of butterflies and riches. Maggie did her homework faithfully. After her labors with Wallace Armistead, she found the regular assignments easy and something of a relief. Before falling asleep, she pored over the Prize List of Wolverton Horse Show. After she had paid for the books, she would still have sixteen dollars and fifteen cents left from her twenty-five dollars. Add to that the three eighty-three she had saved and earned, and that made nineteen dollars and ninety-eight cents. Eight dollars went for entry fees in the Junior Hunter classes, but she still had eleven dollars and ninety-eight cents to divide among classes in the equitation, jumping, and hack divisions. The possibilities of blue ribbons were many and pleasant. Maggie too had happy dreams.

This halcyon time did not end with a bang. It fizzled out. As Martin got closer and closer to the end of Miss Urquhart's collection, and the Armistead letters did not appear, his spirits languished. So did Mrs. Armistead's. She said no more about the pig. The worried lines which had almost disappeared reappeared in Cynthia's forehead. The Wolverton authorities telephoned to say that they were sending a social worker to discuss the case of Miss Urquhart with Mrs. and Miss Armistead. They had found it impossible to deal with Miss Urquhart directly. She was never at home. The social worker arrived with a notebook. She wrote down everything that the Armistead ladies said and seemed to agree with their recommendations. They explained that Miss Urquhart had lived by herself for a great many years and liked it. She was more competent than she seemed. What she needed was financial help so that she could have enough coal for the winter and repairs made to her house. This would cost the town a great deal less than keeping her in an institution. The social worker closed her notebook, nodded, and was about to leave, when Miss Urquhart herself bounded into the drawing room. She carried a bouquet of willow, elm, and poplar, wore a butterfly net like a bridal veil on top of her golden coiffure, and was on her way to the study to feed the caterpillars. As soon as she saw the Armistead ladies and a stranger in the drawing room, poor Miss Urquhart thought that Bugsy's secret was about to be discovered. She gave a yelp of terror and dropped her bouquet. Almost immediately, however, she recovered her presence of mind. Snatching the net from her head and waving it fiercely, she demanded:

"Have you seen it? It came in here. Compton Tortoise. Rare." With a cunning gleam in her lovely eyes, she examined the ceiling, the wallpaper, and tiptoed toward the windows. "Aha!" She jumped high, swung the net, pretended to miss, and tore round and round the room, leaping at intervals, in pursuit of an imaginary butterfly. The social worker froze in her chair while Bugsy called plaintively from the foyer.

"Please, Miss Urquhart, come back. They have company. Please come back."

So absorbed was she in her imaginary chase, that it was some time before Miss Urquhart heard him. As soon as she did, she stopped in her tracks and cocked her head.

"Brain," she explained with a smile of admiration. "Hope of the family." She settled the coiffure, which had been bouncing dangerously as it endeavored to keep pace with the rest of her. "Here I come," she cried gaily, "ready or not," and she skipped from the room.

The social worker unfroze sufficiently to glare long and hard at Mrs. Armistead and Cynthia. She reopened the notebook and made more notes. Finally, she closed the notebook with a snap and took her leave in a manner so bristling that her hostesses knew she thought that they had lied to her, and, worse still, tried to pull her leg.

Soon after this episode, Mr. Purinton began telephoning. Two more companies had announced that they couldn't pay dividends. There was also a matter of taxes. The worried lines deepened in Cynthia's forehead.

Finally Martin came to the end of his search.

"I've been through every paper in her house," he announced to the family at dinner. "There are no letters from Wallace Armistead."

Despite the good dinner, the warm stove, and the spaniels trusting and drooling as always, a shiver ran through the company, as if the chill of Miss Urquhart's best parlor had been wafted into Mrs. Armistead's kitchen.

Bugsy laid down his fork. "In the autumn, I really do expect to be in a position to help her."

"She'll need it," replied Cynthia. With a weary sigh, she bent her head and covered her eyes with her hand.

"Please, Cynthia," Martin begged, "we mustn't give up. You know we've talked about this possibility."

Cynthia lifted her head and managed a faint smile.

"That's better." Martin himself assumed a resolutely cheerful expression as he addressed the others. "Things could be worse. All the authorities say that prosperity is just around the corner. Bugsy is going to be able to help Miss Urquhart, and Maggie is going to win an essay contest and a horse show."

"You don't win a whole horse show," Maggie corrected him.

"Well, whatever there is to win," continued Martin, "Maggie will win it. I must go away for a week or two to see about some business. I have stayed here much longer than I should. I shall miss you all very much. I shall miss our dinners." He bowed courteously to Mrs. Armistead. "I shall be very lonely." He paused, drew a deep breath and finished with another determined burst of cheer. "When I come back, we expect to have a surprise that will make you all happy."

"Who's we?" asked Bugsy.

Martin choked on a sip of water. His face flushed red. "We — " He coughed and sputtered. "We — "

In the act of sneaking a tidbit to Flip, Mrs. Armistead paused and stared at Martin.

"I think he means himself and Emmy," put in Cynthia. She looked at Martin, and suddenly began to laugh.

Flip whimpered. Her tail fluttered. She lifted an anguished forepaw and pressed it on Mrs. Armistead's knee. Mrs. Armistead kept staring at Martin as if she expected him to say or do something extraordinary. Martin got over his choking.

"Yes, that's what I mean," he said. "Of course it is."

Mrs. Armistead sighed and shook her head. "They're too deep for me, Flip," she murmured as she remembered the tidbit and presented it. "Too deep." She patted Flip's head.

The next day Martin was gone.

# 19

Since the other members of her family went about their business with outward calm, Maggie tried to stifle the wild hopes and black despairs which beset her while she waited and waited for the results of the essay contest to be announced. The date of the horse show came nearer and nearer, until it was only a week away. Still there was no word on the contest. Sometimes Maggie almost ceased to hope and fear. The dull misery of waiting muted all other sensations. Elizabeth was her only comfort at this time. If not in exactly the same boat, Elizabeth was in a very similar one. Robert had invited her to the Junior Prom, and her family, obtuse as ever, refused to buy her a black satin evening gown with a low back.

"A pretty, light net or organdy with a round neck, dear," shrieked Liz in hideous imitation of her mother, "will be much more becoming to your complexion, and no one will see how your shoulder blades stick out." Beside herself, Liz screwed up her face and tugged her hair. "I've got to have that twenty-five dollars, and I've got to have it soon. I'll buy a dress myself. I won't embarrass Robert by going to the prom dressed like a baby!" She gave her hair another frantic tug.

Maggie realized that Liz was counting on winning just as much as she was herself, and it occurred to her that, if the suspense went on much longer and Liz went on pulling her hair, she would need a new permanent, possibly a wig, as well as a new dress. Maggie gave herself up to despair. Liz would win. Liz needed the money, and yet, and yet —

Finally, on Wednesday morning (the horse show was on Saturday), a special assembly for awarding prizes was called. The whole school filed into the assembly hall. The president of the Wolverton Women's Club stood with Fried Egg on the platform. Elizabeth communicated her condition to Maggie by rolling her eyes, clutching her stomach, and tugging more violently than ever at her hair. Maggie sat down beside Elizabeth and shut her eyes. Now that the waiting was almost over, she felt so hopeless that she wished the president of the Women's Club would drop dead so the announcements could be

202

put off. All the tortures of uncertainty had been bliss compared to the certain knowledge of failure. The president began a speech. A great many essays submitted — all remarkably good — proud of the boys and girls of Wolverton, etc. — very difficult to choose the best among so many that were good — sometimes impossible — long, deep consideration of problem by board of judges — final decision reached — in classes in which two essays of equal merit had been submitted, the prize money would be divided. Elizabeth poked Maggie. Maggie opened her eyes and watched dutifully while Elizabeth went through the hair-pulling routine again. Maggie shut her eyes. The names of the winners were being announced. She wished she could shut her ears. In the senior class the prize money was divided. In the junior class Robert Appleby was the sole winner. Liz gave Maggie a tremendous poke, and Maggie clapped as hard as she could. Beside her she could hear Liz panting, clapping, stopping presumably to tug hair or clutch stomach, then clapping again. In the next few minutes, while Robert received his prize, and the sophomore winners were announced, Maggie gave up the horse show and the purse of fifty dollars, confronted both her aunt and Fried Egg with the fact that she could never pay for the lost books, and crawled away, disgraced, into a future of shame and remorse. In the freshman class, the president announced, it had again been impossible to decide between two essays, and the prize money was divided between Elizabeth Wheeler and Margaret Armistead.

"Come on!" Elizabeth seized Maggie by the wrist and dragged her, dazed and blinking, up to the platform where she received an envelope containing twelve dollars and fifty cents.

Twelve-fifty subtract eight eighty-five leaves three sixty-five. Add three eighty-three and you have seven forty-eight, not even the eight dollars necessary to enter the two hunter classes. Maggie felt pretty sure that Bugsy could lend her the necessary fifty-two cents, but she must give up all hope of other blue ribbons. It was do or die with the Junior Hunter Stake. She certainly couldn't borrow from Liz. Liz was a little huffy at having to share the prize anyway.

"Oh, I'd rather share it with you than anyone else. After all, you are my best girl friend, but if I hadn't shown you the announcement, you'd never have known enough to enter the contest, and now I've got to find some bargain for twelve-fifty, and I'll probably be reduced to dancing barefoot because I simply won't wear those old patent leathers with the flat heels."

Maggie paid Fried Egg the eight eight-five and left promptly after school to secure the promise of fifty-two cents from Bugsy. Her grandmother and aunt were properly delighted when she told them that she had tied for the prize.

"Dear, dear Maggie!" Her Aunt Cynthia hugged her. "I'm so proud of you. I've always thought that if you only tried, you could be as good a student as you are a horsewoman." She laughed. "Now I know I was right."

She hugged Maggie again. "When can I read your essay?"

"They'll all be in the *Ledger* on Friday."

Now it was her grandmother's turn to hug and kiss her, and she left Maggie quite breathless.

"As soon as Martin explained about your essay, I knew you would win. I knew you had found your hidden ability. Your mother and father were clever, though scatterbrained. Your grandfather was very clever. So, of course, was Wally, poor fellow. You come by it naturally. How I wish they could all know about this. They'd be so proud." The old lady sighed. Her eyes, still resting fondly on Maggie, peered through and beyond her. Her lips moved without sound, and she strained forward as if she were calling into the past, trying to tell Maggie's triumph to all those clever Armisteads who rested in the Family Plot. After a minute she shut her eyes and relaxed. "Perhaps they do know," she murmured.

When she opened her eyes again, they focused firmly on Maggie. "I hope the *Ledger* gives a more prominent place to your essay than to the others. It's important for people to read it and learn the truth. I think I'll telephone the editor now and tell him. Your grandfather owned the paper for years. I should have some influence."

"Oh, Gran, please don't."

"I'm sure they'll put it in a prominent place," said Cynthia, "and just as soon as people see that it's about

205

Wallace Armistead, and that Maggie Armistead wrote it, they'll read it. Don't worry."

"They should," retorted Mrs. Armistead. "Wallace was a very great and unhappy poet, and Maggie is one of the few people who understands him." She turned to Maggie. A smile lighted her face. "No need to worry about entry fees now," she exclaimed. "You can enter Star in anything you like. Run get the prize list and let me look it over. When I thought you couldn't afford to show your horse, I didn't want to see the list or even think about the show." She patted Maggie's shoulder and gave her a little shove toward the stairs. "Now everything is different. Run get it."

Maggie hung back. "I don't think I'll enter her in much."

"Why not?"

"I — I think it costs too much."

"Don't worry about that," exclaimed Cynthia. "You won the prize, and you should spend it as you like." She smiled proudly at Maggie. "You've trained Star to be a very accomplished, well-mannered little horse. I think she will do well. She even has a chance in the Junior Hunter classes."

"I'll enter her in them, but that's all."

"What's the matter with you, Maggie?" demanded her grandmother. "You're not yourself."

The double attack was too much for Maggie. She explained about the lost books.

"I didn't want to tell you because it was a stupid thing to do, and I was ashamed. Please don't feel sorry

206

for me, Aunt Cinny, and give me any money because I know you can't afford to. I've enough for the Junior Hunter Stake, and that's all I care about anyway." Maggie stared sternly, almost defiantly, at her aunt.

Cynthia returned the look with one of gentle wonder. "I don't feel sorry for you, Maggie. I feel very proud of you. Prouder than ever."

"Wait!" Old Mrs. Armistead lifted her cane, flourished it over the heads of Maggie and Cynthia, set it down with a thump, and thumped away up stairs. She returned in a few minutes, took Maggie's hand and laid two silver dollars in the palm. "They're not from me, so don't thank me. They're from Wally. He sent them to us long ago with some clever note that made Henry — but never mind. I've kept them, and now they're going to come in handy. Use them for an entry fee."

"Oh Gran!" Maggie's eyes gleamed.

"Run get that prize list, and we'll decide which class to gamble on. Wally loved to gamble. This will make him happy."

# 20

ON THE MORNING of the horse show, Maggie was at the stable before seven. In the yard, she found Michael already at work on Stardust's coat, which positively gleamed in the sun. Maggie fetched an extra portion of oats for Star's breakfast. While Star munched, Maggie helped to brush her coat and braid her mane. Weeks of planned exercise and feeding had brought Star to the peak of condition. She exuded good health and spirits, and she ate like a pig. Pansy, Bell, and Arrow had lined up along the fence to watch Star's toilet. The two valetudinarians nudged and nodded at each other, a little wistfully perhaps, as if they were reminiscing about the old days when they were the ones to be furbished and polished and fortified with oats and sent out to win blue ribbons for Woodfield. Pansy looked inscrutable, but occasionally her ears fluttered as if she had heard something of special interest.

Carried back to the good old days, Michael actually smiled.

"There she is, Miss Maggie. Couldn't be finer."

He stepped back and studied Star with satisfaction. Michael had never called Maggie "Miss" before. In recent years, as his temper had declined with the decline of the Woodfield stable, he hadn't called her anything but "You" or "Younger Generation." Maggie felt herself endowed with a new dignity, and she tried to be worthy.

"Thank you, Michael, I've never seen her look so fit."

Michael nodded and turned his attention to Maggie's own appearance. "Now, Miss Maggie, if you'll go have breakfast and get yourself washed and properly dressed" — his eye rested meaningfully on the T.R. breeches — "I'll bring your horse up to the front door at nine o'clock sharp."

It was on the tip of Maggie's tongue to say, "Don't bother. It'll take too long," but she stopped herself.

"Thank you, Michael," she replied, "I'll be ready."

Maggie rode Star along the route which she took to school, on through Wolverton Center, and a few miles beyond to a ten-acre field where the show was to be held.

Star was eager and a trifle skittish in the traffic, but she behaved fairly well until, at the ten-acre field, she beheld a great many horses whom she had never met emerging from vans, the like of which she had never seen. She stopped to stare, and Maggie could feel her stiffen. When a horn blew she tried to turn and run for home, but Maggie checked her and made her walk quietly back and forth along the edge of the field. Maggie had purposely arrived early in order to get Star used to the crowd and to take her over the outside course once or twice before the show opened at eleven. When, after ten minutes of quiet walking, Star still went to pieces at close quarters to a van, Maggie gave up on the crowd and trotted over to the outside course. This consisted of eight fences laid out in a rough circle and encompassing a good half of the ten-acre field. First they walked around the course, examining each jump. Except for a spot where the track, descending into a little hollow, disappeared in a patch of alder, turned sharply, and came up to two gates in close succession, the course could not have been easier. Star seemed to have put aside her fears and to be taking an intelligent interest in the jumps. Back at the start, Maggie decided to take her over the course. She headed her at the first fence. Star pranced foolishly, skittered up to the fence, and at the last minute, ran out. On the third try, using her crop with vigor, Maggie got Star over. She lumbered on over the next two fences and the wall in the manner of Pansy at her most uncooperative, and like Pansy bumped to a stop and hung her head. At the distant grinding of a truck in low gear, however, she reared up and tried to bolt. Sick with worry, Maggie clenched her teeth and drove Star at the next fence, beating her as she never had before. Star leaped in terror, tore over the fence, pelted into the hollow, round the turn and up to the first of the two gates. Here she stopped in her tracks, wheeled, and ran for the brush. By sheer good luck, Maggie stayed on. She got Star in hand before they had gone too far, and, repenting now of her cruelty, she spent the next ten minutes walking Star back and forth near the two gates, talking to her, and gently stroking her neck. A voice announced through a megaphone that the show was about to begin and that schooling must stop on the outside course. Maggie trotted Star back toward the ring.

The pick-up truck with Cynthia at the wheel, Mrs. Armistead beside her, and Bugsy, Michael, and an assortment of comforts and goodies for Star in the back, was already drawn up at the ringside. The family waved to Maggie. Mrs. Armistead shouted and grinned. Though her heart was heavy with misgiving, Maggie waved and smiled back gaily. She was grateful at least that the alders had screened Star's performance as she came up out of the hollow. She patted Star, clucked reassuringly, and tried, for Star's sake, to feel calm and confident. Maggie paid her fee for entering Class III for Local Pleasure Horses on which they had decided to stake Uncle Wally's silver dollars. While they waited for the class to begin, neither Maggie, nor Michael, nor Cynthia was able to convince Star that the dangers which kept her jumping and trembling were all in her head. She trusted no one. By the time the class was called, Star had worked herself into a lather. Maggie rode her jittering and skittering into the ring. Her anxious relatives perched themselves on advantageous parts of the pick-up truck and glued their attention on the competition.

"She's the best horse there," declared Mrs. Armistead, "but she's too nervous."

"And Maggie's the best rider," added Cynthia, "but I'm afraid she's nervous too."

Mrs. Armistead replied with a grunt of foreboding.

The other local pleasure horses went round and round at a steady trot, while Star shied and fidgeted among them. When the judge called for a canter, Star leaped too quickly in response to the pressure of Maggie's legs. She got off on the wrong lead, and, only after much fussing, could she be got into the right one. A horse neighed in the distance, and forgetting all her manners, Star tried to run out of the ring. Patiently, Maggie got her in hand and started her again in the right lead. Once more the neigh, far off across the field, galvanized Star, who made efforts to jump the fence. Maggie was barely able to control her. Closer now, like a siren, the neigh rose shrill, slowly faded. Star reared up and neighed hysterically in reply.

In the pick-up truck, Michael suddenly emitted a rasping cry and made frantic efforts to climb out. A moment later, as the neigh rang out close at hand now, Mrs. Armistead, Cynthia, and Bugsy caught their breaths at once and scrambled as best they could to the ground. They were all too late. Pansy, halterless, breathless, but pigheaded as ever, rushed a man who had the temerity to try to stop her, sailed over the fence, and joined Stardust in the ring. Star's joy knew no bounds. She nudged and nuzzled and playfully kicked up her heels at her old friend. After the chums had romped their fill and completely disorganized the other local pleasure horses, Pansy allowed herself to be tempted by Michael and a plate of oats. She was led away in a borrowed halter, and the judging was resumed. Needless to say, Star won no ribbons in that class. But that was not the end. Michael had no sooner got Pansy tied up to a tree in a quiet corner of the field, than Bell and Arrow hove into view. Red in the face, and muttering a diatribe against ponies, Michael, with more oats and more borrowed halters, hobbled out to meet the aged couple as they hobbled in. He escorted them to Pansy and the tree. The whole Armistead party gathered around to help revive them. Bell and Arrow hadn't walked so far in ten years and were very nearly prostrated. Star, momentarily forgotten, stood quietly beside Pansy and watched the oldsters being walked and rubbed and offered refreshments. As he worked, Michael kept up his diatribe, mostly in an undertone, but occasionally bursting out loud.

"You opened the gate yourself. You know you did, you lying, cheating, stunted, underbred abomination, unworthy to be called horse." He shook his fist at Pansy, who turned her back on him and nibbled nonchalantly at the bark of the tree. Star loyally turned her back too, and laid her chin on Pansy's neck.

The elder, livery-stable Crosby now joined the Armisteads. Though old and fat, Mr. Crosby senior waddled all the way from the ring to pay his respects to his old friend Mrs. Armistead. George, he explained, had driven him over in a Chrysler 80 which he was displaying at the ringside as an advertising venture. The elder Crosby was in high spirits. It was a long time since he had had the pleasure of seeing so many horses and discussing them with Mrs. Armistead. At lunchtime, he did full justice to her sandwiches, which the others were too agitated to enjoy.

At 2:30 the entries were called for the Junior Working Hunter Class. Maggie pulled her hard hat firmly down onto her ears and mounted Star. The moment she was in the saddle, she felt that Star was quieter. They trotted to the In Gate of the Outside Course and, along with six other entries, waited their turn. Star pricked her ears and looked about with interest but no trace of fear.

"I think she's steadied down," Maggie called to her aunt, who was walking with the others to a good position at the edge of the course.

Cynthia smiled. "Maybe Pansy's coming wasn't such a disaster. Good luck!"

# 21

THE CROWD was moving over from the ring. With it
came George Crosby, particularly noticeable because on
his head he wore a handkerchief knotted at the corners
as a protection against the sun. He did not join his father and the Armisteads. He did not even nod to them,
but strolled along the edge of the course looking over
the jumps. Suddenly, to her surprise, Maggie recognized
Liz and Robert approaching hand in hand. Liz waved
frantically. Robert waved more sedately while the sun
flashed from his spectacles. Maggie started Star forward
to meet them, but, at that moment, the first entry was
called. Forgetting everything else, Maggie turned her

attention to the course. A pretty chestnut gelding ridden by a girl about Maggie's age cantered out, headed for the first fence, and at the last minute, with a shrewdness worthy of Pansy herself, slithered off to one side. In three tries the girl was unable to get the chestnut over. The next entry was called. This one did well on the first three fences and the wall, but refused point blank to have anything to do with the two gates at the top of the hollow. As Star continued to stand alert, but quiet, Maggie felt new hope swelling in her heart. The fourth entry, however, gave her pause. The horse was a big rawboned brown creature with one blue eye. The rider was a bony boy with enormous feet which protruded along with an expanse of leg from the bottoms of his jodhpurs. Both horse and rider looked comical until they began to jump. The horse moved with precision and grace, and, in action, the boy became as precise and graceful as his mount. They were a magnificent, inseparable team as they sailed over the first four jumps. They disappeared in the hollow, reappeared twice, briefly, flying high above the screen of alders as they cleared the two gates with room to spare. They breezed over the last two fences and drew up, amidst clapping, at the Out Gate. Maggie clapped too, in admiration, but she knew now that she and Star must do their utmost to win. They cantered out, circled, and approached the first fence. Maggie's legs pressed against Star's sides. She held the crop ready, but she didn't need it. Star wanted to jump. They cleared the first three fences and the wall. As they approached the fourth fence Star was tearing on so fast that Maggie had to hold her back. At the last minute, she let her out again, and they flicked over in style, cantered down into the hollow, and then, as if reminded of her morning's fears, Star faltered. Maggie clucked, drove with her legs, and as Star jumped, swung forward with her, almost lifting her over first one and then the other gate. Star's hoof ticked the second, and although they completed the rest of the course perfectly and received applause, Maggie knew that they hadn't won. The remaining entry was of no account. The bony boy with his blue-eyed horse got the blue ribbon. Maggie and Star got the red.

Although she admitted to some disappointment, Mrs. Armistead assured Maggie and everyone else within range of her powerful voice that it was no disgrace to place second to such a horse and rider. The horse reminded her of one she had owned in 1913. The elder Crosby remembered that horse too. They discussed it point by point. The younger Crosby strode off toward the hollow. It was almost as if his father and Mrs. Armistead offended him so with their loud talk that he wanted to get out of sight and hearing. Maggie took Star over to Pansy to rest until their next class was called. She did not feel like talking to anyone. She and Star had done their best and been beaten. That was it.

The hundred-dollar Junior Hunter Stake was called within the hour. Once more Maggie and Star waited their turn at the In Gate. There were ten entries. The first three did well, then the bony boy and his horse came out and completed the course without a serious mistake. Maggie was one of the last to be called. As she cantered through the gate, she felt that she hadn't a chance, but, as Star pricked her ears and gathered herself for the first fence, Maggie forgot her worries in the pleasure of jumping so willing and accomplished a horse. They took the first half of the now familiar course in high style and cantered into the hollow. Whispering encouragement, Maggie pressed Star a little harder, until she saw George Crosby pop up from the alders just ahead. George's head was now bare. He held the knotted handkerchief to his nose as if he were about to blow it. His sharp little eyes gauged Maggie's approach. Suddenly he seemed to lose his balance. Throwing out his arms as if to regain it, he tossed the knotted handkerchief across Star's path. It floated down like a parachute. Maggie shouted in alarm. For a second Star hesitated, then putting her whole heart in the effort, she cleared the two gates without a jerk or a hitch in two smooth, perfectly timed leaps. Star had skipped over the last jumps and slowed obediently to a walk at the Out Gate before Maggie fully understood what had happened. An official from the judges' platform was running toward the hollow shouting to George to get away from there. Didn't he know he might have caused an accident? With a flash of certainty Maggie knew that George did know. That, in fact, was exactly what George had intended to do, but Star had mistaken his handkerchief for a butterfly and Maggie's shout for the cry of the chase. True hunter that she was, Star had given her all to those two gates. Maggie bent forward in the saddle and lay with

her arms clasped around Star's neck while she called
her every endearing name she knew, laughed shakily,
cried a little, and wiped her nose and eyes in Star's mane.

George, making hearty apologies, was escorted to the
Out Gate by the enraged official.

"Just wanted a good view of those two hard gates.
Suddenly had to sneeze. Well, no harm done." He
trained his friendliest smile on the knot of spectators
gathered there and chuckled. No one smiled back.
George's smile faltered. Deliberately avoiding the cold
eyes of his father and Mrs. Armistead, he cast one last
furtive glance over the silent crowd and scurried away
to the protection of the Chrysler 80.

Maggie accepted the blue ribbon and the fifty-dollar
purse, but she reiterated to everyone who came to congratulate her that it was Star and Star alone who de-
served the credit.

Liz, with Robert in tow, dashed up to Maggie and
embraced her.

"You were simply marvelous. We both think you
were simply marvelous. Don't we, Robert?"

Robert blushed. Shyly he smiled at Maggie and
opened his mouth to speak.

"Robert is absolutely crazy about you and your
horse," exclaimed Liz before Robert had been able to
produce a sound.

Robert blushed redder. He managed to emit an eager,
but inarticulate cry before Liz silenced him.

"We both want to learn to ride. Don't we, Robert?"
She gave Robert time for one quick nod and tore on.

"You must give us lessons, Maggie, and we'll pay you because we've changed our minds about how we're going to spend our money. Robert isn't going to run away and be a hobo, and I'm going to do without a black satin. I want to buy riding clothes instead because I think they're so divine-looking. Will you give me lessons, Maggie? Will you? I know I'll never get to ride so well as you do, and I probably won't look nearly so chic in my riding clothes, but I want to learn. I really do."

This torrent left Maggie stunned and giddy. She rested her head against Star's neck to steady herself. Hardly able to believe her eyes, she noted that, through his spectacles, the exalted Robert was regarding her with a sort of dazzled reverence. Proud Liz was waiting anxious and humble for her, Maggie, to deliver judgment. Maggie felt a warm glow of happiness well up inside her.

"Sure I'll give you lessons, Liz, if you want me to." She smiled at her friend.

"Angel!" Liz blew her an ecstatic kiss. "And Robert? Will you give him lessons too? He's absolutely dying to learn."

Robert took a quick step toward Maggie. "Will you? Will you?" He choked on his eagerness.

"Sure I will," replied Maggie and added in the fullness of her own happiness, "It won't be long before you're both good riders."

Robert's countenance glowed. He drew a long breath preparatory to speech, but was cut off once more, this time by a shrill and anxious call.

"Maggie, Maggie!" Bugsy ran up, panting. "Listen, Maggie, you and I have got to lead home Bell and Arrow. It'll take forever, and I'm worried about my caterpillars. I want to get back to them."

"What's the matter with them?"

"I don't know, but something is happening to them. I've got a premonition. Please come, Maggie, please."

"O.K." She patted his shoulder. "I'll be right along." She nodded to Liz and Robert. "I'll have to ask Gran about horses for you and how much to charge. I'll tell you at school on Monday."

Leading Star, she followed Bugsy to the tree where Pansy, Bell, and Arrow waited. Pansy had been rigged up with a borrowed bridle, but as no pony saddle could be found with a girth long enough to go around her, Bugsy rode bareback. They proceeded very slowly in order to put no strain on Bell and Arrow and stopped frequently to let them catch their breath. The sun was low by the time they had deposited their charges in the stable. Bugsy made immediately for the house, but Maggie helped Michael put the horses to bed. Michael was positively genial.

"You can't beat the Woodfield horses," he said, and, quite openly, he gave Pansy such a large helping of oats that she uttered an astonished whinny. "Nor the young ladies and gentlemen either," continued Michael, distinguishing Maggie with a nod of approval which left her as astonished as Pansy. "There's a young man at the house now," he went on. "Maybe he's not so handsome nor so wild as Mr. Wallace or poor harum-scarum Mr.

221

Henry, your father, but times have changed, and the young men have changed with them." He shook his head, not in disgust, but in resignation. "He needs grooming and schooling, but he can be made to do." Michael chuckled. "I say you could look farther and do worse." He winked at Maggie and led Arrow into the paddock.

Maggie started toward the house wondering if Michael had lost his wits. When she spied Emmy under the porte-cochere, she forgot Michael and broke into a run.

## 22

MARTIN!" Maggie burst into the foyer. "Did they tell you? We made it. We won. Martin!"

Martin and Cynthia hurried out from the kitchen, and Martin lifted Maggie off her feet and swung her around. "They told me. I knew you could do it. You just needed confidence."

"It wasn't me. It was Star."

Martin dropped her and held her off at arm's length. "Are you trying to tell me that your horse wrote that essay for you?"

"Oh that." Maggie tossed her head. "Who cares about that? I mean the Junior Hunter Stake."

Martin and Cynthia laughed while Maggie glowered at them.

"Don't mind him," Cynthia patted her arm. "He's just teasing you."

"Forgive me," begged Martin. "I know Star was magnificent, and you too. Cynthia told me. I tried my best to get here in time for the show, but Emmy had three flat tires."

Maggie was mollified. "I'll tell you about it."

"But first," Martin interposed, "we have something to tell you." He took Cynthia's hand and drew her close beside him.

"Wait, Martin, we must tell Bugsy too. We mustn't leave him out. Where is he?" Cynthia turned to Maggie.

"He's around somewhere. Bugsy!" Maggie shouted in the general direction of the study.

There was no answer.

"Bugsy," called Martin, "we've got something important to tell you."

No answer.

"Bugsy," called Cynthia.

Still no answer.

Suddenly, breaking the stillness with its brassy, penetrating clang, a clock struck six times. Cynthia's face went white. She gripped Martin's arm.

"It's Father's clock. Something is wrong." She dragged Martin with her across the drawing room and down the passage. They threw open the study door to discover Bugsy in the act of shutting the pendulum case of the grandfather clock. In his hand he held a wad of yellowed paper with a caterpillar perched on top. His eyes were popping right out of his head.

"Bugsy, what are you doing?"

"Please, please don't come in." Bugsy thrust out the wad of paper and the caterpillar in a gesture of supplication. "Don't squash them. Please don't. I'll explain everything, but please don't walk on the floor."

"What is it? What's the matter? I heard Henry's clock." Mrs. Armistead drew up behind them. Her voice quavered and almost broke. Her hand on her cane trembled.

"Don't come in, Gran. Wait at the door. I'll explain everything. Just don't walk in and squash them." Carefully balancing the caterpillar on the wad of paper, Bugsy began to pick his way on tiptoe among the countless caterpillars that were crawling purposefully over the study floor. Bugsy reached the door, stepped out, shut it behind him and leaned against it.

"They're not just crawling around for fun," he said. "They're looking for a place to pupate in."

"Bugsy Armistead," shouted his grandmother, trembling more violently, but with anger now rather than fear. "What do you mean by touching your grandfather's clock?"

"I'm trying to explain," said Bugsy. "They're all looking for a place to pupate."

"Bugsy Armistead" — the old lady raised her cane — "if you try any more tomfoolery with me, I'll beat you."

"But Gran!"

Maggie took her grandmother's arm. "Let him explain, Gran."

Mrs. Armistead lowered her cane. With a jerk of the head she commanded Bugsy to explain.

Bugsy launched into an account of the butterfly farm. While he spoke eloquently on his favorite subject and held his astonished listeners enthralled, he never forgot the caterpillar in his hand, and he twisted and turned the wad of paper in order to keep the caterpillar on top.

"I didn't want to open the clock, Gran. I wouldn't have touched it if there had been any other way, but I could see this caterpillar," and he held it out to her, "hanging on the pendulum. It must have crawled under the case and up the side and then down the pendulum. It wanted to pupate there, but I couldn't let it do that. When it hatched, it would beat itself to death against the inside of the case." He fixed his eyes on his grandmother. Two tears welled out and rolled down his cheeks. He wiped them with the wad of paper. "I opened the case and reached for the caterpillar, but I fumbled, and it fell down inside. I reached down inside for it. Luckily this bunch of paper was down there, and the caterpillar had landed on it. Otherwise I might have squashed it bringing it up. Then I bumped the pendulum, and the clock began to strike." Bugsy shut his eyes. "If I hadn't had this caterpillar to consider, I'd have fallen over in a dead faint. I was so scared."

For a few minutes Mrs. Armistead simply stared at her grandson. "A butterfly farm in Henry's study," she muttered, and, as if overcome, she leaned against the wall, and she too shut her eyes.

"I think Father would have approved," said Cynthia suddenly.

Mrs. Armistead continued to lean against the wall, but she opened her eyes.

"When I heard that clock booming out after ten years of silence, I felt as if Henry himself were booming something at me out of the grave." She shivered and shut her eyes again.

"And in a way you were right," suggested Cynthia. "He was booming approval of Bugsy's butterfly farm."

"Not in his study. Not in his clock." Mrs. Armistead shook her head.

"Perhaps Father wouldn't have picked the exact place Bugsy did" — Cynthia bit her lip — "but Father was a businessman. The butterfly farm is a business venture, and a very successful one." Cynthia looked hopefully at her mother, but the old lady did not open her eyes and continued to shake her head. "It was you, yourself," urged Cynthia, "who said that all the Armisteads had hidden talents and Bugsy's was a talent for business."

Mrs. Armistead opened her eyes. "Did I? I didn't realize what he was up to."

"You know very well that if there was one thing Father admired it was a talent for business. He didn't care what sort of business, or where. He was booming approval. I know he was."

"I hope you are right, Cynthia. I believe you *are* right." Mrs. Armistead gave a sigh of relief, but turned on her grandson. "Business or no business, Bugsy, that clock is not to be touched again."

"I hope" — Martin smiled at Mrs. Armistead — "that Cynthia and I may consider the booms as approval of our marriage as well as of Bugsy's business."

Mrs. Armistead considered this possibility.

"I see no reason why he shouldn't approve. He's had plenty of time to cool off and feel sorry after that last temper fit of his, and when he gets to know you better, Martin, I think he'll realize that you are quite an enterprising, businesslike young man. His first impression of you, I remember, was good. It was just his jealousy of — " She realized that both Martin and Cynthia were smiling affectionately at her. "I'm a foolish old woman. I get the past mixed up with the present. At any rate," she declared, "I approve, and Henry usually came to see things my way in the end." She embraced first Cynthia and then Martin. "Now I must get back to my engagement dinner before it spoils."

"What engagement dinner?" demanded Maggie. "I should have thought it would be a Junior Hunter Stake dinner."

"Cynthia," exclaimed Mrs. Armistead, "haven't you told the children?"

"Maggie," said Cynthia, "I was just going to tell you when the clock struck. Martin and I are going to be married."

Maggie looked at the floor and did not reply. Cynthia took her hands.

"We hoped you would be glad to hear it."

Maggie still looked at the floor. In a muffled voice she asked, "Will you go away?"

"No, of course not," cried Cynthia. "We'll stay right here. Martin has a job in Boston."

"That's why I left two weeks ago," explained Martin, "to look for a new job. Your aunt wouldn't marry me unless we could go on living here and looking after you and Bugsy."

"I couldn't leave you," said Cynthia. "You know that."

"I didn't know," replied Maggie. "I didn't know anything about it."

"I did," said Bugsy. "At least, I guessed." He turned to Martin. "We'll be glad to have you in the family. We need another man around the place. You are the best that's turned up.

"Thank you," said Martin.

"That's all right," returned Bugsy. "I'll teach you about the butterfly business. I'll be needing some help."

"Thank you." Martin smiled at Bugsy, but his eye wandered uneasily to Maggie, who still stood with bent head and held her aunt's hands awkwardly as if she was afraid to be seen holding them and afraid to let them go. "If I'm going to be in this family, I think I ought to know something about horses too." Martin hesitated. "I thought that maybe Maggie would teach me to ride."

"You could learn," interrupted Mrs. Armistead with decision, "and it would do you a world of good. You must make Cynthia ride again too. It will do her a world of good." Mrs. Armistead had forgotten about her dinner. "Cynthia, I think Mr. Roote could help me find some nice quiet saddle horses, nothing expensive, as a sort of wedding present."

Maggie lifted her head.

"Do you really want to learn to ride?" she asked Martin.

"Yes, I really do."

"Then I'll give you lessons free (I usually charge) because you are one of the family."

"Dear Maggie!" Cynthia hugged her black head. "You always do what's best. You always make me proud of you. It's not just I who will be happy because I marry Martin, and he stays here with us. We'll all be happier. You'll see."

"It's not that I don't like him," exclaimed Maggie, "because I do. I was just afraid —" She stopped short and sighed. "I was afraid you'd go away, and I felt bad because I hadn't noticed about you and Martin, not at all. I guess Liz is right about me, but, well" — Maggie reached in her breeches pocket, and her face brightened — "I may not have known about it, but I've got a wedding present for you." She proudly extracted her prize purse and held it out to her aunt.

"No, no!" Cynthia pushed the purse away. "You mustn't give me your prize money. You won it. It's yours."

"Star won it, but it's a wedding present from Bugsy and me. We've been planning this for months, only we thought it would be a birthday present. Bugsy will give you his half as soon as his butterflies hatch and he sells them. We want you to buy back Amber, or, if that's too expensive, any good horse, so you can ride again."

"You've got to take it," said Bugsy, "and in a few weeks there'll be more."

He looked fondly down at his caterpillar who was still wandering over the wad of paper. His eyes lighted with happy inspiration. "Here, Aunt Cynthia." He thrust the caterpillar at her, wad and all. "Take this as a sort of down payment on what's coming. I'll get a jar for it. You keep it in your room and watch it." He ran off to the kitchen.

With the purse in one hand and the caterpillar in the other, Cynthia smiled in happy confusion first at one present then the other, until the caterpillar made a sudden descent into the folds of the paper.

"Martin, he's disappeared. Please get him out. I'm afraid he'll get hurt."

While Cynthia held the wad, Martin began to open and smooth out the papers. The caterpillar had fallen deep into a crevasse. Fearful of hurting it, Martin worked with great care. Suddenly he caught his breath. His hands hovered trembling over the half-opened wad of papers. Cynthia looked down and saw it, too. Across one of the papers, unmistakably bold, careless, and clear, was scrawled the signature of Wallace Armistead.

It is to the credit of both Cynthia and Martin that, as

231

they sorted out the various pages of Wallace Armistead's letters, they did not forget the caterpillar and injure it. It was safely deposited in the jar which Bugsy brought from the kitchen. The letters were spread out on the drawing room table.

"They are the very ones he showed me," said Martin in an awed whisper.

Mrs. Armistead spoke slowly and, for her, softly as she reconstructed the last moments of her husband's life.

"He was waving them around when he shouted at me. I went to wash my hands, then I went to the kitchen. While he was waiting for me to come back and listen to him, he remembered that it was time to wind his clock. It was hard to do with one hand, so he crushed up Wally's letters (he was still in a rage) and dropped them down inside the case. He wound the clock, shut the case, and because he didn't feel well, he went to the door to call me, and that was the end." She wiped a tear from her eye, blew her nose, and looked to Cynthia for corroboration.

"Yes," said Cynthia. "That is what must have happened."

Maggie examined the letters.

"With these, I could probably write an even better essay."

"That's just what I was thinking of doing myself," said Martin. "Would you be interested in collaborating?"

"Yes, if you want," replied Maggie, "but first you should learn to ride. Gran, call up Mr. Roote right now and ask him about a horse for Martin, and then let's call up the people who bought Amber and find out how much they'd sell her back for."

Mrs. Armistead nodded enthusiastically. "I will, my dear, just as soon as — Good heavens! My dinner!" She started for the kitchen. "Maggie, Bugsy, you come and help."

The children followed her, leaving Martin and Cynthia alone to examine their latest wedding present. It was so exactly what they wanted, and had been delivered by such devious means from the depths of time, that they could explain it only as a token of affection and esteem from the immortal Wallace Armistead.